KRISTÍN ÓMARSDÓTTIR

Kristín Ómarsdóttir is the author of novels, poetry, short stories and plays. She has won numerous awards including the DV Cultural Award for Literature, the Icelandic Women's Literature Prize and the Icelandic national prize for playwright of the year. She has been nominated four times for the Icelandic Literary Award and twice for the Nordic Council Literary Prize.

Vala Thorodds is director of Partus Press and managing editor of *Oxford Poetry*. She is the recipient of a PEN/Heim Translation Fund grant and her poetry and translations have appeared in the *White Review, Guardian, Granta* and *The Penguin Book of the Prose Poem*.

T0322038

KRISTÍN ÓMARSDÓTTIR

Swanfolk

TRANSLATED FROM THE ICELANDIC BY
Vala Thorodds

VINTAGE

1 3 5 7 9 10 8 6 4 2

Vintage is part of the Penguin Random House group of companies
whose addresses can be found at global.penguinrandomhouse.com

First published in Vintage in 2023
First published in Great Britain by Harvill Secker in 2022
First published with the title *Svanafólkið* in Iceland by Partus in 2019

This book has been translated with a financial support from:

 ICELANDIC LITERATURE CENTER

penguin.co.uk/vintage

Printed and bound in Great Britain by Clays Ltd, Elcograf S.p.A.

The authorised representative in the EEA is Penguin Random House Ireland,
Morrison Chambers, 32 Nassau Street, Dublin D02 YH68

A CIP catalogue record for this book is available from the British Library

ISBN 9781529115710

Penguin Random House is committed to a sustainable future
for our business, our readers and our planet. This book is made
from Forest Stewardship Council® certified paper.

In memory of my brother
Árni Björn Ómarsson
19 September 1965–19 June 2018

BY THE WATER

27 March–7 April

Prologue

I came from a country that didn't exist and lived from birth in its capital, by a blue bay and a violet mountain whose slopes were scaled by a verdurous green in summer and in winter were veiled by snow. Over the land drifted sublime clouds, and the damp, rocky soil gave rise to vegetable patches that yielded mighty potatoes. On the horizon the sun curtsied politely like a chorus girl. In foreign lands she disappeared behind apartment blocks and high walls but it was the Atlantic Ocean that served as my country's border wall, though the winds refused to acknowledge this. Lakes and rivers were clear and crowded with trout, droughts unheard of, the mountainscapes a tangible mirage. Light ruled the skies in summer and ceded to darkness in winter.

My house stood on a hill above a cove in the bay. From my bathroom window I could see the famed mountain whose colour shifted endlessly in the changing light, a motion picture projected onto an enormous screen.

My parents, Unnur Rósberg and Rúnar Björn, devoted their lives to languages. They disappeared at a symposium abroad when I was twelve years old. It fell to my grandmother Elísabet Unnur Rósberg to teach me to care for and tend to my body, which she did without instilling in me the shame that so often gets passed down like a dowry. My parents believed the body operated on autopilot, which language distorted or disturbed. In a handbook for writers, authors are encouraged to cite their mother or another guardian sooner rather than later, to strengthen the credibility of their narrative and honor those who came before. I quote at random from a letter that Mum wrote to Dad when she was carrying my brother, Unnar Björn, her firstborn, four years my senior:

The mother tongue's capacity to describe the machinations
of power and the nuances of oppression is so limited that
the child will never be capable of articulating its captivity.
Rúnar, how will our child ever be free?

My grandmother had since been gathered to her ancestors, and my brother, who worked as a guide on top of a glacier in three-week shifts, lived with his fiancée, Þorsteina Margrét. I suspected Unnar of being a pyromaniac, because once when he was a teenager Grandma and I saw him set fire to his guitar on the balcony while the sun was setting. I presumed that was why he chose to work on a glacier.

Ever since we were little we imagined we had a sister, whom we named Æsa. 'What do you think Æsa is up to now?' Unnar and I would ask each other when we spoke on the phone. 'She's searching for us,' one of us would reply – and we believed that one day she would find us, and we her.

Formal Beginning

Each weekday, as I arrived for work at the Special Unit at the Ministry of the Interior and greeted the guards by the security gate at the back of the grand and refurbished lobby, I looked forward to bidding them farewell in the evening and heading off on my daily walk beyond the city. My walks often dragged on so I packed provisions, leftovers from past meals. From an early age I sought out experiences that could not be described in words. I don't know whether on my walks I felt *joy*, *calm*, *intimacy*, *peace* – all beautiful and appealing words, but the feelings didn't know their own names when I interrogated them:

How do I feel? What is this feeling called?

One day, early Sunday evening, just as the late-winter sun was setting, I sat on a green bench by a green lake at the base of a forest on the outskirts of my young and fair city and thought of nothing, just practised inhaling and exhaling deeply. I hadn't yet touched the food in my blue satchel – which wasn't quite blue, rather more grey, but in any case slim and light. Perhaps I dozed off for a moment there on the bench. It wasn't like me to doze in the open, but I can't rule out the possibility that it could have been a dream.

On the lake I spotted swans. Or rather, creatures with the hybrid form of swan and human. I took off my glasses and raised a pair of binoculars to my eyes:

One creature bounced a fishing line in the water, another washed her hair, others swam the evening rounds like townsfolk milling about in warm summer twilight. Yet the earth was still frozen underfoot, as befitted the season. Suddenly one of the creatures swam near, stepped onto the bank and showed herself to me – her lower half that of a thickset swan, the upper half that of a regular-sized human. At the pond in the centre of town I sometimes fed the ducks. I dug into my satchel and threw some bread her way and she gobbled it down. The rest of the provisions from my bag soon disappeared into her and her companions, who swam over. The one on the bank made what appeared to be a gesture of thanks, slipped back into the water and swam off. The flock crossed the lake and disappeared behind a thicket on the far side.

A pair of ravens flew east towards the hills beyond the lake, their final reconnoitre before turning in for the night. The traffic on the highway skirting the lake to the south and west had calmed. I shook off my stupor and marched in the direction I had seen the creatures disappear. A human couple ran past me wearing skintight sparkleclothes and trainers, with red and yellow hats and mittens, earbuds in their ears. For a moment I thought I saw silver tails hanging from the backs of their trousers, swishing to the rhythm of their run. When I reached the opposite side of the lake I took a seat on another green bench.

Cars speckled the highway yellow and red, forming tender

streaks in the dusk. The reflective material shimmered on the clothing of the runners, who were now passing the bench I had sat on earlier. A sudden rush of whispers filled the air – a female voice began to sing, and more voices joined in for the chorus.

The runners nodded as they passed me again, then disappeared behind a bend in the path. I seized the opportunity and followed the sound, crawled under a thicket, then another. There, in a forest glade, a group of swanfolk sat singing around a pyre, playing dented guitars, a bruised trumpet, ripped drums, a ukulele. I counted twelve of them.

And as I lay there under the trees, listening to this mighty choir, I fell asleep. An hour or so later I was awoken by a cold quiet. The scent of an old fire hung in the air but nothing was visible except darkness, and I was afraid of the dark. I couldn't distinguish between myself and my surroundings; I feared my inner demons would escape and attack me from without, which was worse than their attacks from within. I worried, too, that I'd caught pneumonia, jumped to my feet, and knocked into a spruce tree; birch trees scratched at my face. Mercifully the city's maintenance staff had installed lampposts along the path around the water. Grateful to them and for the electricity, I walked back the way I had come and crossed the empty highway. A pair of headlights snaked their way down the mountain, which blended with the sky and marked the formal beginning of the countryside. Once home, I lay down in bed – which was wine-red like my and Unnar's childhood bunk bed – and doubted everything I had seen. Surely no one would credit the word of a person who had fallen asleep under a bush.

Flower

During the night a flower grew in my throat, and by midday it had bloomed. For the next five days I was unable to go to work because of a cold. Once the flower had wilted, shrivelled, died, and buried itself in my digestive tract, I quickly forgot the long, tedious days spent browsing the web and playing video games. At work I had been assigned a report on stand-up comedy in the city, and I went online in the hopes of familiarising myself with the wider scene. It ought to have been enjoyable to watch stand-up routines for eight to sixteen hours a day, but my spirit languished.

When I was back on my feet and getting ready for work I looked for my satchel and wool hat but couldn't find them anywhere. It seemed that sleeping out of doors like a bird of passage entailed losses both physical and financial. Bagless and hatless, I waited for the bus in a red shelter two streets over, by a lamppost with a sign displaying the timetable. Every morning I imagined a dog, Rex, waiting with me at the stop until the bus appeared and he ran off into a field behind the shelter. In the wind he could run around to his heart's content, snapping at his tail and the fresh outdoor air.

After work I bade farewell to Adda and Jónatan, the husband-and-wife security guards in the ministry foyer. Adda and I admired the new floor. Nowhere else could you hear such a beautiful indoor echo, she said, and I agreed and set off on my walk. My stamina had taken a hit, but I didn't spare myself and walked breathlessly to begin with. I half-ran across the highway to a chorus of car horns, cursing the rush-hour traffic.

From the green bench I soon moved down into the grass and threw stones at the water. Not intentionally to disturb the stillness that lay like a blanket over the land, but involuntarily, to fill the silence with a rhythm. I didn't manage to skim the stones. Perhaps I knocked out a few plankton. Personally I wouldn't have minded if a giant troll pummelled me with rocks from atop the mountain, or a polar bear appeared – grsesgrsjgrsjiiíjjíí – and tore off my arms, my head, and devoured my memories. I was indifferent to so much and yet averse to catching pneumonia. The contradiction in my character was heartening – to want to be eaten alive at the same time as shielding myself from infection.

A group of people ran along the path in grey and yellow glitterclothes – colleagues? spouses? a running club? What did it matter? My involuntary analyses of everything I witnessed were like annotations in the margins of my mind, and they riled me. Within me slept a desire to disconnect from this day and age even as I surrendered to its siren song and dutifully played my part as a disciple of its staggering mechanism – whose charms, however, did not conceal the fact that its temptations led one unequivocally to destruction. If I spent my free time almost exclusively outdoors, walking, I would have fewer opportunities to lose myself in such temptations. Just then I heard a rustling. From the reeds emerged a creature of the kind I had met about a week earlier. She handed me my bag, the blue-and-grey one.

'You forgot it,' she said in my language.

My heart raced as I accepted the bag from the hand of a creature half human, half swan.

'Wait,' I said, and looked in the bag. 'Did you by any chance see my hat?'

She turned around, catching me in the periphery of a glance whose horizon was wider than that of human eyes. I felt embarrassed. The creature seemed to look right through me.

'No.'

'Who are you, may I ask?'

'I am no one and belong to swankind. But who are you, if I may, Miss Human?'

'I am also no one and belong to mankind. My name is Elísabet Eva.'

'And my name is Ástríður Petra.'

'How are you able to speak a human language, if I may ask?'

'How are you able to?'

We both shrugged. Then she stuck her tongue out and said: 'Idiot.'

I said: 'Little shit.'

She: 'Pig.'

At that she ran away as quickly as her short legs could carry such a heavy load. A creature of the swanfolk line disappeared behind a hill. I followed her at a short distance, found a clearing on the other side of the hill and more bushes, and behind one of them another clearing concealed by spruce and birch. But I didn't trust myself to go any farther. I vaguely remembered having been sick and that I needed to take care, yet I wasn't in the mood to go home. I decided instead to go to A&E and have my head examined. I squeezed the bag that this morning had been lost to me. The city's security cameras could confirm that I had come to the lake bagless and walked back with a bag on my shoulder. Had customs officers been posted at the city limits, as the new municipal plans proposed, they could have corroborated that fact.

Accident & Emergency – Opening Gambit

In the waiting room's glass cage, under the *Reception* sign, I presented a white girl in a white uniform – wearing gold-rimmed spectacles and a gold necklace – with an ID badge that gave me priority ahead of the lines at the hospitals. In the waiting room a group of men stood on crutches with their arms in slings, and three dust-covered men sat on a bench with yellow helmets in their laps, drumming their fingers on the domes. On another bench a dark-clothed woman sat in the arms of a dark-clothed man and hid her face in a yellow towel. From the bathroom came the sound of retching, and an incessant voice imploring: 'Darling, just try to swallow it, just try to swallow the vomit.' To the other visitors I must have looked like a representative of the government on urgent business, due to my taupe trench coat – our uniform at the Special Unit – and like the rest of my colleagues I banked on the visual implication.

A nurse with a mask over her nose and mouth appeared in the electric doorway and ushered me inside. Warmth radiated from the eyes of the doctor – whose name was Dóra but whom

I called for no good reason Doctor Bónus – as she listened to the descriptions of my hallucinations: that I had walked beyond the city to a green lake, met strange beings, half human and half swan, that I was completely sober, hadn't had a drop to drink or taken sedatives or opiates during my recent cold. Dr Bónus sent me to the radiology department. There I lay down inside a camera that sketched out my brain with rays while I was tasked with holding my head still in a steel helmet under a steel cupola, supine and restrained on a blue bench with wrist cuffs and a tube attached to a needle stuck into a vein on the back of my hand, through which the developing liquid spurted. Under the rumbling of the ray-pen I sang the anthem of my homeland and other patriotic hymns.

After the imaging I waited for Dr Bónus on an orange chair in a room with blue shelves and a sink. The radiologist's preliminary examination indicated a healthy cerebral hemisphere, she announced as she came in to discharge me. During one half of the moment I bade farewell to my sister, Æsa, while the other half dissolved into froth. I felt dizzy. I felt I had entrusted a double agent with my visions and now she would send my employer an unfavourable report. The fear wasn't entirely unfounded. But my intuition assured me that this was exactly the right move: to go to A&E and inform the authorities of my hallucinations.

Behind the City Hospital, home to the most advanced accident and emergency department in the country, on the frontier between sickness and health, I waited for the bus in a red shelter that, like the bus shelter back home, recalled the letter boxes that once hung outside the neighbourhood shops, the so-called corner shops, in the times when letters still went around in envelopes. Now I would send myself home like an enormous letter.

According to the new municipal plans, a checkpoint was to be built on the plot of this shelter, staffed by border patrol officers, just like at the National Hospital. On the gable end of a block of flats I counted forty balconies and windows – ceiling lights on in five of them, lamplight in three, a television in one – and didn't hear the young man walk into the shelter, I who had immaculate hearing and ought to be vigilant at *every* moment. He wore a red anorak, had a backpack on his shoulders, buzz cut, wide face, sunken eyes, burst lips, congealed white froth in the corners of his mouth, and his bruised, swollen hand held a bouquet of flowers. He asked me where I was from.

'The city, and you?'

Poland.

He asked me how old I was; I answered and asked him back. 'One hundred and forty-nine years old,' he said, then apologised, one shouldn't ask about age, age is irrelevant, and he proposed to me, said he was tired of girls, that one had so few people one could talk to – he felt he could talk to me. I said I would never get married.

'The two of us are lonely,' he said, and I agreed. We introduced ourselves: Elísabet Eva, Lúkas.

'Many girls in Poland are named Eva,' said Lúkas, and added that women choose men, not the other way around. Men choose women for one night, two at most.

'Oh, is that how it is?'

'Yes, that's how it is.'

The bus came to a halt in front of us. Lúkas stayed behind in the bus shelter.

'Viva la revolución,' I said as I stepped onto the bus.

'Easy for you to say,' he said, and waved the bouquet as I took my seat and the bus pulled off. At my stop, Rex fawned over me before disappearing down into the heath. If they found nothing else remarkable on the brain scans, I would trust reality. But which one?

Under More Measuring Devices

Tuesday afternoon, I bade farewell to the golden couple, Adda and Jónatan – and their son, Burkni, who was studying for his finals in the back room behind the security gate. I buttoned up my coat, placed a new yellow beanie on my head, secured my thermos, binoculars, leftovers, journal, blanket and torch in my bag, and suddenly started to worry that my preoccupation with walking might interfere with my ambitions at work – which, in my case as in many others', served as a kind of axis in my life. The couple smiled so pleasantly that my worries dissipated and I marched off in my new hiking boots, crafted in the Alps. Several horns snorted amid the din of traffic as I darted across the highway separating city and countryside.

The weather was fine, cold, mild; the sun shone.

The raven couple on duty was flying the day's final reconnoitre. Ravens went early to bed. My new boots improved my walking pace; I felt like an owl who had borrowed an extra pair of wings from a falcon. I came upon a path snaking up the slope and wandered into a forest. The trees on the front lines stood guard and examined me from every angle, appraised automatically the threat my journey posed – they scanned me more precisely than any man-made machine could, their arsenal better concealed than my own. Confident of my innocence, I drifted onward without mapping the way, found myself a clearing and spread out the striped blanket that Grandpa had once given Grandma as a birthday present. I lay down in the grass and ate an apple. The trees continued inspecting me with their flawless equipment.

She Isn't Well,
the Human Is Suffering

'The human isn't well,' Ástríður Petra shouted as she towered over me. The creatures stood clustered around. I counted seven of them – swans below, humans up top, with female breasts under their jumpers. One wore a yellow cardigan that appeared to belong to a label favoured by my boss Selma Mjöll. Some weeks earlier we had no doubt flipped through a fashion magazine at her house and admired a similar garment.

'I feel fine, thank you all for your interest,' I corrected them. 'I'm just resting after a long walk before heading home. Are you going to introduce me to your friends, Ástríður Petra?'

'She's not well,' Ástríður Petra repeated. They leaned over, slid their palms under me and carried me out of the clearing. 'She's not well,' echoed another, 'She's not well at all,' repeated yet another, 'No, she's not doing well,' they muttered.

I was too polite to ask where they were taking me. In a basic training seminar, which covered responses to the unlikeliest of situations, I had not learned how to react to a group of swan-dames lifting me up and carrying me off. Surely I couldn't disturb their ritual with a reaction like fear. This could turn out to be the opportunity of a lifetime, for me and for the Special Unit, and truth be told I felt both at risk and at peace there on the air stretcher.

We came to the next glade but two or but three – I didn't count them as we passed and instead placed my trust in my internal compass.

'She's not well,' they muttered, 'what can we do?'

'Give her something to eat,' said one, 'let her swill from the breast. But there isn't any godforsaken milk in our breasts. She'll have to drink something else.'

'Why isn't there any milk in your breasts?' I said, full of curiosity.

'That's because, Elísabet,' said Ástríður Petra, 'we are decrepit old swandames who worry about everything and everyone.'

'Oh,' I said, identifying with her anxiety. 'You know, the antidote to worry is trust.'

'Oh, you must be joking,' they laughed.

'Yeah.'

'Because you're like us – you trust no one.'

'True,' I muttered.

They laid me on a heap of down and covered me with my grandmother's blanket, which an eighth creature carried in her arms.

'Sleep now for a little while, soon Mummy will come with milk for the sad girl,' growled another swanmaiden in a monstrous voice, then tore off my glasses. Still I refused myself the luxury of being afraid. Everything was as it should be and couldn't have been better. I was out in the open air, mixed up with a mysterious and strange realm of which few stories existed – certainly none that I had heard, and I was meant to be better informed than most of my countrymen in fundamental matters of human life in the under- and overworlds and all the worlds between.

Conversations over Supper

While pretending to sleep I listened to the humming and murmuring and heavy-footed bustling around the nest. If I opened my eyes one of them was there to close them again, so I gave up on trying to peek and enjoyed my captivity. They spoke a language that my parents would have liked to study – never had I heard such squawks and rasps, melodies that did not belong to any known tonescape. How I wish I could describe it precisely. The smell of a bonfire and burning flora filled my senses. They woke me, though I was already awake, and gave me back my glasses. Supported by swandames, I stepped out of the nest. A pyre blazed and the trees were decorated with rubbish, lanterns and ribbons; plates lay on a chequered cloth, and bowls were filled with deep-fried roots, lamb droppings and twigs, bones, fishes, grasses, moss, worms, sand eels, frozen berries and many other delicacies. Nine swanladies sat around the fire, made room for me and offered me a seat. Cats with luxurious furs walked around and grazed against us, seemed to be waiting for the leftovers – or for something, at least. Soon night would fall. I would never be home before dark.

They told me to help myself and I took a sand eel for my plate.

'We know who you are,' announced a creature whom I decided to call the leader, since she sat higher than the others, on pink cushions, wearing ski goggles. 'You've been showing up around here lately to spy on us for the city authorities. What's the plan? Are we to be exterminated?' She swallowed a sand eel whole, her fingers adorned with rings and her·wrists with bracelets. Before I spoke I also swallowed a sand eel whole.

'There is talk of moving you to the City Zoo,' I answered boldly and without thinking. The idea came to me from nowhere, but later it would turn out not to be so far-fetched. Several of them laughed, the leader included, but Ástríður Petra scolded them and said:

'At least there we would be fed daily, receive medical care, shelter and protection. And we wouldn't have to hide – in fact, we'd show ourselves off to the visitors.'

'We don't know where we come from originally,' explained the one who sat beside me in the yellow cardigan, with purple eyelids and red, diamond-shaped lips, whom I learned was called María. 'Whether our foremothers and forefathers fled here in the spring and couldn't be bothered to return in autumn, or they got stuck here because of the weather – we can't say – or why we live by the lake, but it's all we know, and we're just as blind as you humans when it comes to seeing into the future. Oh, wouldn't it be nice to see into the future?'

'Yes and also back in time, because we have no historical sources and no one taught us anything about the past,' said

Ástríður Petra. 'We were very young when everyone died, which is why we don't know the first thing about anything.'

Ástríður's cap had 'Paris' written on it. Other swandames also wore baseball caps, balaclavas, fur hats, beanies with and without tassels, and hats with brims.

'How did everyone die?' I said.

'We just told you that we don't know,' Ástríður Petra said. 'Suddenly everyone was dead except us kids.'

'And maybe no one died,' María added. 'Maybe they fled in a panic.'

'Maybe they hid us and were going to come back. Maybe they'll come back for us and take us to the promised land,' added another, who introduced herself as Soffía. 'We wish we could tell you about them but it's impossible, we can't remember that far back.'

'We come from nowhere,' one of them said, ringlets dancing around her head. 'We are landless, come from nowhereland. Countrylessduckskulls loose facelessspiritless nowhere now here nowhere now here, nowhereless and penniless too, we come from nowhere –'

María took hold of her hands: 'Relax, my dearest darling.'

'I'm so cold,' the other replied, 'but words warm my frosted heart and fingers.'

'Same with me,' I said. 'I was born in this beautiful country, which is seemingly nowhere, and spend my life saving for an old age that for all I know may never come. Maybe the planet will stop in its tracks. Maybe the sun will have it stuffed and mounted. Maybe the sun will have a heart attack.'

'Ach, yes,' said María sorrowfully and yawned.

'Ach, yes,' said Ástríður Petra and sighed.

'Is your name Æsa?' I asked one of the others. She had grass-green eyes and eyebrows that met in the middle.

'Kornlilja,' she said. 'We also think it's beautiful here.'

Another swanmaiden spoke up: 'Yes, a very beautiful country, though cold.'

'We are both *urbis amator* and *ruris amator*, am I right?' María asked and looked expectantly over the group.

'Exactly right,' replied Ástríður. 'Although we know next to nothing, we do know a few words in Latin. By the green lake we endure bliss and terror in equal measure – so it goes,' she added and nodded. 'That's life, the bliss and the terror alternate.'

The one with the ringlets repeated: 'Bliss and terror, brrrrrrr, terribly cold – terror – bliss, brrrrrr, so blissfully cold – the bliss and terror can't tell each other apart but everyone knows that one starts with *b* and the other with *t*, brrrrrr, so terriblyterriblycold.'

'What is your name, if I may?' I asked.

'We call her Blíng,' a few answered in chorus.

'Blíng,' repeated Blíng, and she acted as if she were being tickled all over. Her curls twirled around her head like horses on a merry-go-round.

From the bowls they picked out and ate dried blades of grass, worms, fry and twigs, and I followed suit, reached into the bowls for grass, worms, fry and pinecones.

'I'm Lena,' said Lena while applying lipstick, 'and I would

gladly live in the City Zoo. There we'll meet other animals, and
we could delight the children who come to visit. We haven't
had any young in a number of years.' She looked into my eyes
the way people do when they want to affirm the truth of their
words. 'Yes, we certainly do miss the young, we love children
and nestlings,' she added and offered the lipstick to Kornlilja,
who also applied it.

'Children are the future,' Blíng crooned, 'we adore and l o v e
children, children are the future, brrrrr, if no one is born we'll
go extinct and then there'll be no need to wipe us out – out, out,
out, out, out, out, out, out, brrrrr, so cold . . .'

'Relax, my precious darling,' María pleaded and wrapped her
arms around Blíng, who leaned against her. 'The cold unsettles
her, our dear Blíng.'

Ástríður Petra whispered in my ear. 'Blíng is the youngest
and the best. She's anxious because she and Órekur, her fiancé,
have been losing eggs for a few years now. If she lays eggs at all,
which is never certain, they perish in the cold, the Easter chill,
the Maysnow. Our foremothers didn't anticipate how horribly
cold this country could get – how could they have known?'

'Oh, yes, the Maysnow,' I bleated, and felt as if I were naming
a type of cake you could buy at the bakery. Then I sighed and
wrapped my arms around my stomach, a movement that was
automatic and meaningless but which the swandames fixated
on as though my abdomen were a window on the future.

The leader spoke up: 'My girls, what should we do, die out
or have the chance of a future for our species in the City Zoo,
where our eggs will be allowed to hatch in optimal conditions?'

'Pride kills, servility offers a future,' María muttered. 'Best to bring about a dignified end, to terminate the species's earthly existence and autonomy with beauty, style and grace.' With her index finger she drew a line across her neck.

'Bring about a dignified end, live beautifully, and do it with care, with care,' Blíng sang with her eyes closed, the merry-go-round switched off.

'I can't tell the difference between a proud slave and a proud master,' Lena said.

'Me neither,' said Soffía.

'I can see the difference,' said María, 'but I can also see how the difference is distorted with every passing hour.'

'I want to be on display,' Lena insisted.

'Me too, I *want* to show myself,' added another, who introduced herself and offered me her hand: 'Hello, Elísabet, my name is Kósetta.'

'I too am tired of hiding and staying out of sight on sunny days when the kids are out biking and going on picnics, and on the days when the cleaners from the city show up, spraying poison for pests and destroying everything they consider old, dingy and ruined, in their tireless effort to sanitise and sweep the area for explosives,' Ástríður Petra said.

'I like not being seen,' muttered María. 'I feel best behind the bushes. I w a n t to hide, I don't want to be seen *a t a l l*.'

'I am unseen: I *am* not. I am seen: I *am*,' Soffía shouted with her index finger aloft.

'You have such beautiful eyelids,' I said, pointing at María, 'and you, Kornlilja, and you, Kósetta, and you, Lena, and you, Soffía, and . . .'

'I DEMAND to be seen,' huffed Lena.

'I want to be on display, visible – visible – miserable – visible,' sang Blíng, who also had beautiful eyelids, cheeks and rings under her eyes. She had upturned eyelashes and furry ears from which earrings hung like glimmering anchors.

'It's a terrible burden to not exist,' explained Lena in anguished tones.

'Yes, I've read a lot about just that,' I said and took off my hat so María could brush my hair. 'We pawns need acknowledgement, otherwise we don't know whether or not we exist and so feel like shadows. Birth certificates are a necessity, but so are the affirmations of existence that go beyond mere bookkeeping. The unofficial officiations. Every individual is born both formally and informally, and both versions of the self, the formal and the informal, play equally important roles in a person's development. This I read –'

For a moment I doubted my standing within the group. After an uncomfortable silence, the leader nodded: 'That's right, and for this reason one must respect one's shadow and give it as much attention as one's body.'

'Spoon-feed the shadow with candy,' Blíng yelled and stuck her thumb in her mouth.

'I adore having a guest who says "what beautiful eyelids you have." Then one is really alive,' Lena said and winked at me.

'Me too,' said Soffía.

'Me too,' said Kósetta, 'it's a fine thing to be alive and to be there for others.'

'Not me,' said María, 'not at all. The guest's preoccupation with her hosts' appearance fosters inequality and invites division.'

'I find that interesting,' I was going to say.

'I don't know whether I want to be seen,' said Kornlilja, and she closed her eyes in the same way my sister Æsa might have done. A lively fringe spilled over her forehead. She shuddered. Kornlilja was cold, too. The leader raised her hand, blew a whistle, and said: 'We're not complaining, but female mammals *never* find earthly purpose, formal or informal, except in the moment when their offspring kicks off its shell – am I right, girls?'

I wanted to ask whether they could be classified in the order of monotremes, as they laid eggs even though they lacked beaks and their breasts were no secret, but Ástríður Petra said as assertively as the leader: 'None of us left alive have managed it, but all our thoughts and deeds aim toward this one goal: to give meaning to our lives by multiplying our precious stock.'

Blíng sang and rocked herself: 'We are orphaned, unfit, orphaned and hungry motherkin, sterilised of all purpose.'

María finished brushing my hair and asked the ladies whether they liked my do. They complimented the hairstyle, said that I was a sight to behold, then said nothing while they chewed and swallowed loudly. Some of them choked on the food and coughed it back up, spat up shreds of their dinner into their palms and then swallowed them again.

Lena coughed and said, 'Funny how the soft worms stick in your throat.' And she drew out a long earthworm and showed it to us. It was clearly their sport and amusement to swallow worms whole. Much as I tried, I couldn't do it. I spat out the worm and apologised. Ástríður Petra grabbed the worm and swallowed it with panache as the rest cheered her on. Some of them roasted the worms with tongs over the fire and warmed up little bundles that they had packed with pine needles, grasses, worms, shredded pinecones and dried insects.

'Do you find us strange?' said Soffía, who took off her hat, adjusted a yellow headband embroidered with gardenias, and put her hat back on over it. She was wearing a very beautiful wool jumper.

'No stranger than what comes and goes. I've probably seen stranger table manners among humans.'

This made them sad.

'Don't compare us with humans,' María said and put on yellow sunglasses.

'It's a strange thing to be half human and miss the other half, to be half swan and miss the other half,' the leader explained. 'It gives rise to a complicated emotional life. Sometimes we think like humans even while we feel like birds, think like birds but feel like humans – we are jealous of swans, jealous of humans; despise swans, admire humans. Admire swans; despise humans and swans equally. Humanswans like us will never fit the mould.'

Blíng hummed: 'Fit, unfit, fit, unfit, fit, fit, unfit, fit.'

María stroked the back of Blíng's hand.

'Yes, I recognise the feeling though I am entirely human,' I said, and considered the taste of a pinecone.

'Aha,' said Ástríður Petra with her tummy full of worms (she wouldn't touch anything else), 'you humans pretend to understand everything, but you don't understand shit.'

I agreed with her, endowed as I was with the ability to agree with most things, a quality I was praised for when I finished top of the class in Anthropology of Feelings, a required course in basic training.

'At the end of the day it's probably not much fun to fit the mould,' said Kornlilja and blew her nose into a yellow hand-kerchief, which she then handed to María, who also blew her nose and handed the kerchief to the swanmaiden Mandý, who blew her nose too before offering the hanky to Kósetta. Never before or since had I seen anyone blow their nose with such artistry.

The leader turned to me. 'Calm yourself, dear, you don't have to prove yourself to us. We know how worthless you are and that you want to make amends for your worthlessness with obsequious and sycophantic attempts at charity. We also know that you are going to sell us out to our enemies, in order to shore up your rusted bank account – and we will forgive you, because we understand you better than you understand us.'

'Ouf,' I said, floundering for a response. 'I won't sell you out to anybody.'

Then they laughed heartily and the fire highlighted how many of them were in need of dentistry. My brother's best friend was a dentist.

'My brother's best friend is a dentist,' I said. 'He would be happy to come to the lake and examine you. I would pay for the repairs in full, also for caps and titanium screws.'

In my head I calculated the average cost and then multiplied it by nine. I compared the sum to the balance of my savings account A, which I had opened in case of unexpected hardship, unlike savings account B, which was devoted to my old age.

A hush fell over the group.

They spat onto the fire and it dimmed. The wind aided their efforts, rushed through the glade and swept the flames off the lanterns hanging from the trees. Everything became dark and suddenly cold, as during a solar eclipse. The creatures brayed. At the exact moment they charged at me I received an accurate premonition and jumped to my feet with my bag aloft, fumbling my way through the dark – but Ástríður Petra grabbed the heel of my shoe and we wrestled for my foot. Lena snatched at my coattail, which tore, and an unknown hand with long nails grabbed at my ear. My shoe came off, enabling me to break loose, and I rushed out of the glade and off.

In the Lorry

The trees clawed at me as I ran – into a tree trunk and then another and down the hill, through dips and hollows and clearings wearing one shoe and along the path around the water – then I clambered up the gravel leading to the highway, flagged down a lorry and climbed into the cabin. The driver was thin and short. For a split second I felt like he was driving a doll's car, even though the tyres' height exceeded my own. Inside the cab it smelled of pink Bazooka gum and bright washing powder. The man repeatedly bit his purple lips. On the radio a singer crooned over wind instruments:

I am not a character in a novel
not a character in a novel la-la-la

How Blíng would relish singing in a studio, her eyelids draped over her dreaming eyes:

I am not a chess clock, not a chess clock
but a swan and a woman with no need to checkmate a tale
that I don't belong in at all la-la-la

'Is there something I can assist you with, my dear driver?' I shouted over the din of the engine.

'What's that?' the driver shouted back. He wore a wool jumper similar to that of the swanmaiden Soffía.

'Are you in financial trouble – does the driver need money?'

'No, not at all,' the driver shouted, 'I'm doing just fine, thank you; the economy is in a major upswing, as is consumer spending.'

'Good to know,' I shouted. 'So lorry drivers have it pretty good in the boom?'

'Never better, thanks to the unions,' he shouted.

'Handed in your tax return?'

'Oh yeah, a while ago.'

'Oh good, very good.'

I pulled out a sandwich from my bag.

'May I offer sir a bite?'

'No, thank you, I couldn't. Just had battered fish at the Little Café.'

'Is there some memorial fund or savings account the driver knows of that the undersigned could make a deposit into?'

The lorry danced onto the hard shoulder while the man looked at me. Luckily he was able to steer it back between the lines and avoid an accident.

'Are you off your rocker?' he said and bit his lips; he was missing one of his canines.

'No more than usual,' I shouted and turned off the radio. 'You at least know a kind person who has knitted you this magnificent wool jumper, unless of course you knitted it yourself.' I inspected the pattern on the jumper as if I were an expert.

'My sister knitted the jumper and gave it to me for Christmas. Just do me a favour and get your shoes sorted,' he said, 'then I'll be happy. Find the other shoe or buy a new pair.'

'Thank you for the sound advice,' I said, 'spoken like a true Buddhist. One's most important possessions are one's shoes. One's primary mode of transportation.' I turned the radio back on.

The next song was about drifting along as if in a fairy tale.

The man snuck a peek at me the way a tree examines another tree, then dropped me on the kerb where I asked him to let me out: on the side of the road below the bus stop at home. Rex ran down the hill, licked my foot, jumped into my arms and licked my face, then took off across the highway and disappeared between some buildings in search of a bone.

On Good Old Boozer Square

After work on a perfectly pleasant Wednesday that did little to distinguish itself from other days, I couldn't be bothered to go buy myself a new pair of shoes like I had promised the driver; it would have been extravagant to buy a new pair so hastily, and for all I knew the missing shoe might yet turn up. In the storeroom at home I found a pair of rain boots unscathed by time, from the collection of my grandmother or my mother or my sister Æsa. They proved useful in the overcast and windy weather. It was snowing when I walked out later that afternoon in a different direction than usual, not east but west, downtown, and stopped on a bench by Parliament Square, a notorious refuge of drunks, where I waited for some external force to pull the rug out from under me.

I sought intimacy. Meaning. Human chaos. I wanted to listen to the wisdom of people with unwebbed feet who had drunk all sense away, the weight of whose words is such that one feels immediately unburdened. According to research that had not yet been carried out, the words of a person who has lived through more trauma and had a worse life than the average person (than the majority) are sharper than those of someone who has lived in ostensible safety. A man wearing a blue snow suit walked straight and tall onto the square and sat down on my bench.

'How do you do. I don't know your name but I knew your mother,' he said. He was a man of inscrutable age, but I assumed he was younger than me.

'My name is Elísabet – may I know the gentleman's name?'

'Arinbjörn. But most people call me Raccoon, because I'm considered tidy for a drunk.'

'How did you know my mother, may I ask?' I said, curious and up for a good time.

'She was a dear friend and important to me – helpful, warm, and sympathetic.'

'How so?'

Arinbjörn, or Raccoon, leaned in: red stubble on his weathered skin; high cheekbones; one eye green, the other yellow; the veins around his eyes flushed with blood. Before I drew back I noted his dental hygiene.

'Your mother was a good listener, sincere, compassionate. That's also why her life became so difficult.'

Because of an intolerance to eulogies I interrupted him: 'No, friend, you are mistaken. My mother had a happy life until she disappeared at the symposium.'

'Yes, but her journey was often difficult and she was certainly unjustly treated, and misunderstood by most.'

'What injustice did she suffer?' I said, grimacing.

'You don't know what you've got till it's gone.'

I was furious. '*You're* telling *me* that?'

'Yes.'

'And where is your mother?' I said coarsely.

He gestured with his eyes towards the hilltop cemetery on the far side of Parliament.

'Ugh,' I muttered, 'you lot sure do make martyrs of women.'

'What?'

'All that talk about how dames have it bad and are slowly dying of their own kindness and sympathy. It would be an understatement to call your talk arrogant. Why should women be so sympathetic?'

'Now listen here,' Raccoon said, 'are you going to tell me your mother didn't suffer?'

'I don't know about your mum but my mum enjoyed life to the fullest, researching languages.'

'Have it your way, dear,' Raccoon said.

'Yes, thank you,' I said, 'I will. With or without your permission.'

We took turns swigging from a bottle of vodka he drew from one of the many pockets on his snow suit. Finally, in the frigid mist – which, farther off, hid Parliament from our view – I couldn't hold back any longer.

'My brother's best friend – well, my brother's friends are my friends, and had I friends they would be my brother's friends too – but this particular friend is ready to assist me with most things, naturally, in order to be there for his best friend's little sister, not because he owes me any favours but because he's a good person and a dentist. Anyway, because you say you knew my mum, I want to invite you to go to my brother's friend for dental repairs, which I will pay for in full, no expense spared.'

The man's expression warned me to make myself scarce before things turned ugly – but I didn't, since we had an equal right to sit on the bench, both being holders of the country's passport. Before he doled out the punch he slowly pulled off his tattered mitten, his fingers branded with the letters *h-a-t-e*, alongside a wedding ring. Unfortunately Raccoon was left-handed; he hit me with precision and walked away buoyantly, with the bottle in his back pocket. I stayed behind on the bench and thanked myself for not needing to cry, looked up to heaven and prayed:

Dear clouds, please bring me rain.

And instantly it rained. Then snowed.

I stood up from the bench, keen to avoid catching a cold in the wet weather, walked home with my tail between my legs. Some are tickled, hysterically or delicately, if a tail hangs between their legs, but because I lacked the need for love and possibly because of a false nature I felt nothing, neither a tickle nor humiliation.

Called onto the Carpet

On Thursday morning I began the day by tidying my desk in the open-plan office of the Special Unit, on the third floor of the Ministry of the Interior. I was about to empty my wastepaper basket when I received a summons from my boss to come directly to her office. Calmly I put on the cardigan draped over the back of my chair, hung up my bag under my most prized possession, the trench coat – towards which I felt the way a patriot must feel about the national flag – emptied my trouser pockets of a pencil stub, hair tie and handkerchief, and laid them all on the desk along with my phone, which rang. Green letters formed the word *Brother* on the screen. It was soothing to watch a phone ring out, like standing on a riverbank watching a boat pass by and not waving.

Were any one of us in the unit called in to see Selma Mjöll Ófeigsdóttir first thing in the morning, that individual could expect rebuke, criticism, reproach, even dismissal. Her favourite color was red. She alone wore a red overcoat, while the coats of her subordinates and our other boss, Helgi Björn Björnsson, were taupe. Her hair was shoulder-length, large spectacles balanced on her eagle nose, her manner seemingly free and modern. She was easygoing and carried herself with a practised informality that allowed her to joke with her subordinates in a spare moment over the Danish pastries served on Fridays. I acted as if I were expecting a promotion, walked tall into the meeting, trailed by the eyes of my colleagues: Was it Elísabet Eva's turn?

My boss and I were compatible on the dance floor despite our height difference. In the world outside of work, such as at the dance classes we attended from time to time, we called ourselves Rósa and Frankó.

Rósa: 'Hello, Frankó.'

Frankó: 'Hello, Selma – I mean Rósa,' I replied, and sat down in the chair that Selma had pointed to. She complimented and enquired about my hairdo. I said I had done it myself. She found that strange. I said that it wasn't strange. She asked me to take off my sunglasses.

'Drop the act, Elísabet,' she added when I resisted. 'We heard about you downtown last night on the boozer benches by Parliament Square, talking to the soon-to-be most notorious city bum of summer 20XX, Raccoon' (she was reading off a screen), 'baptized Arinbjörn Arinbjarnarson, born 15 April . . .' Selma leafed through some papers on her desk. 'What was being discussed so intimately?'

'My mum,' I answered conscientiously, and switched out my glasses.

'What are you saying – did the man know your mother, Unnur?'

'So it would seem, however that may fit with reality.'

'Elísabet, you are too valuable an employee to be drinking from a bottle with a bum downtown. All of my employees must exercise extreme care and hygiene in both work and play.'

'Apologies, I won't make a habit of it.'

She switched her reading glasses for her nearsighted ones, brought her hands together and focused her intense gaze on me.

'That's a hideous black eye, dear.'

'I offered Raccoon free dental work and reaped this in return. What man wouldn't sock it to a strange woman who talks about his missing teeth?'

'Ouf,' said Selma and clutched her mouth.

'You have beautiful and whole teeth,' I promised.

'Why did you offer to pay for this man's dental repairs?'

'I wanted to do some good.'

'That's a nice thought.'

'To say my life is egocentric is an understatement,' I added with the intonation of an automaton.

'You're not alone there,' Selma said and switched glasses again, looked through some papers.

'I've discovered that the alienation felt in our society is caused by the old idiom having been inverted: *It's better to receive than to give.*'

'Interesting idea. Would charity also improve this weather?' she said, leafing through more documents.

'You never know,' I replied, and couldn't stand my own cockiness, looked at the scales on the bookshelf, wrought in copper and iron – gorgeous old scales that weighed the balance between capital and democracy in the country. 'Today they tip considerably in favour of capital,' I diligently pointed out.

'Yes, right – don't stress me out, Beth. We need to file a report this afternoon to the minister about how we can right the imbalance as quickly as possible.'

'With a referendum?' I asked, and was about to mention an idea that had recently occurred to the unit's democracy task force at one of their weekly brainstorming sessions, that it might be possible to balance the scales with a referendum: actors from the national theatres would nominate themselves for the role of Hamlet, the citizens would vote among the nominees – but I couldn't get the words out because I was awaiting further scrutiny. Selma answered my question with a question of her own about how my assessment of the stand-up comedy scene was going, while closely examining a pink sheet of paper. The ink must have been invisible, because as far as I could tell the page was blank.

'I have finished about two-fifths of the report.'

'Do you expect a tenable conclusion?'

'It's not as simple as it first seemed. We also need to look at the influence of foreign stand-ups.'

'We are most interested in the content, not the form, remember –'

'But these foreign comics are often courageous, and bravery is infectious.'

'Yes, I'm afraid that's true – just be careful not to bite off more than you can chew, Elísabet.'

'I'll be careful about that,' I replied, then added, 'Selma Mjöll.'

'Remember last year?'

'I haven't forgotten.'

'Is the end-of-times anxiety coming back at all?'

'I hope not.'

'The spring is a sensitive time.'

'Can I do something for you, Rósa?'

'Like what, Frankó?'

'Rub your shoulders . . . run to the shop . . . do you want some crisps?'

She looked like she was about to laugh and maybe it occurred to her to say something like she never ate crisps in the morning. Instead she asked me for four sentences from my report so she could introduce it at the meeting with the minister. Selma knew shorthand and typed as I spoke:

'The local comics go to the swimming pool on the same day they perform on the city's various stages, large and small; the men are either closely shaven or their beards neatly trimmed, hair freshly cut, conventional clothing, shirts ironed, T-shirts with a picture or an advert, polished shoes, white trainers, hiking boots; dresses and skirts are rare, even among the women, unless the garment enhances their exuberance.'

Selma raised her hand like a crossing guard – in the summers during college she had worked for the traffic police – and ordered me to file the report in a week's time, on 14 April. She looked at the calendar, was going to press the red button with her index finger, her long nails brilliantly red, but looked up instead, switched her glasses and gave me a leaden stare: 'Elísabet,' she said, hesitating briefly. 'You know how hard it is for me to occupy a seat of power.'

'Yes,' I answered and nodded as if to express how familiar I was with the topic.

'And how I avoid thinking to its rational conclusion how much I enjoy controlling people and seeing the consequences of my orders. But I am also good at it, as we know. Yet sometimes one gets tired, as is human, and when I get tired I think of you –'

'Why?' I said, curious and astonished.

'Because in your company I become normal.'

'Because in my company you can act how you like?' I said cautiously.

Selma laughed. 'Exactly what I mean, Elísabet – around you I become calm.'

'Calm-er,' I corrected her.

'Calm-er,' she added, and I wanted to say that I didn't get the joke – which is to say that it wasn't a joke – but I couldn't be bothered.

'When I boss you around I *act* like your boss, but I *am* not your boss. Do you understand the difference?' she said and waved her hand in the air, her bracelets rattling. She pointed to my ear, said that I had a scrape. I shrugged. She moved her finger to the red button, pressed it – her nails fire red – the doors whistled and opened, and as she strutted to the front of the desk her heels clicked wonderfully on the floor, steps that would rather have danced the short distance. She wanted, I think, to show me her new clothes: a wine-red V-neck dress, green suede shoes with a little heel; a necklace on which hung a globe-shaped pendant, and I knew who had given it to her –

given her the world, the whole world – but I would, as I should, keep that to myself. Like a true subordinate I bowed, swapped my clear specs for the tinted pair, and walked out of the office, the glass doors closing behind me. The image of the catwalk model began to fade but I held on to it, a bit longer than my mind wished.

Ástríður Petra &
the Bookswan, Álfrún Perla

The blue-grey bag hung faithfully on my shoulder as I strode
off more optimistic than usual and almost like a toy soldier:
with a black eye the world is one's oyster! Dressed in Grandma's
(or Mum's or Æsa's) green rain boots, I gave myself a pep talk,
a prayer we had been taught in the academy to recite before
setting off on a mission.

From Isaiah 54:17:

> No weapon forged against you will prevail, and you will
> refute every tongue that accuses you. This is the heritage of
> the servants of the Lord, and this is their vindication from me,
> declares the Lord.

Across the highway that separated civilisation and wilder-
ness I ran between a cement lorry that drove *away* from the
city and a cargo van that drove *towards* it, and felt as if I were
meeting my parents again – my mother the cement, my father
the cargo, or the other way around – and slipped on the loose
gravel beside the highway, rolled down increasingly large peb-

bles into the field below. I sniffed, smelled, inhaled the ground in this order: sniffed, smelled, inhaled – took off my sunglasses, looked to the sky, pretended to smell the blue air, pretended I could get a whiff of it, mmm – the blue – yum yum – what do you taste like, my dear blueness?

For a gratuitous moment I wanted – despite a general lack of desire and need for love – to *make love* with the ground and the sky – which was the mum? – which was the dad? – the ground the dad? – the sky the mum? – the other way around? – or interchangeably? – such trite and airless daydreams! I bit my tongue, plucked a stalk of sedge and chewed it.

The lake sparkled.

A swan flew across it.

The trees and bushes didn't stir; neither did the reeds. Last summer there were bluets growing in the field and I picked some and gave them to Rósa, and I would have written a poem about the flowers and given it to her along with the bouquet, had I been a poet. But I wasn't a poet. Would the poem have ended up in the same bin as the bouquet? Would she have forgotten the poem but remembered the look of the flowers? Was it possible to write a poem about the interbreeding of hand and mind, earth and heaven?

'Oh, you again –' said a voice behind me. 'You dared come back here despite everything? What an eyesore you are, human!'

'I was punched last night by a tidy drunk, as he described himself,' I said and put on my sunglasses. 'But he had full right to hit me as I had crossed a sacred line, and in that regard I had failed to learn my lesson from our meeting the day before yesterday: one should exercise caution in the company of another soul.'

'Must be edifying, being punched by a drunkard,' said Ástríður Petra.

'You don't meet better or more levelheaded people,' I replied arrogantly. 'Drunkenness and disorder, if regular drinking can be called disorderly, is virtue's purest and sincerest reply to the cruelty of the world. But in my country, in this respectable country of mine, intellectuals don't even know the name of the god of wine, so deep is the prejudice and so poor is the spirit,' I muttered on.

Ástríður Petra pulled me to my feet.

'And why would the gods bother to protect love in a country where men break faith with the knowledge that ale has its own god and protector? No, my fellow countrymen refuse to acknowledge that the gods have never differentiated between love and drink . . .'

I followed Ástríður Petra, who sauntered regally down to the water and jumped in.

'The god's name is Dionysus,' I said, 'if you care to know. That is to say if you didn't already . . .'

She swam in the direction of the green bench on the other side of the lake and stepped up onto the bank. I followed her around and up the hill until we reached the glade. In a big heap of a nest there lay a large furry egg and on top of the egg sat a swandame, covered with my grandmother's blanket, reading a book. Thankfully I bit my tongue before I could ask whether she was literate.

'My name is Álfrún Perla,' she said and smiled, 'and this is a wonderful book I'm reading. It's about a spy called Issa

Blóðberg who is tasked with keeping an eye on the schoolmistresses in the city, monitoring whether they work by the rules, attend to their duties, and stick to the curriculum. Have you read it?'

'No,' I said, 'may I see the cover?'

Álfrún Perla threw the book at me. It was laminated and bore the seal of the National Library. The cover featured an aerial photograph of the city and in the top right corner there had been spliced an image of a person flying, wearing a trench coat very similar to my own. I turned the pages of the book at random and read:

'The train sped off, with our heads on the luggage racks within, out of the city, away, away, away. *All or nothing, all or nothing* sounded from horns high up on the streetlamps. In the afterglow we stood headless on the train platform and waved goodbye.'

'Must be an interesting read,' I said and threw the book back to Álfrún, who caught it.

'Very,' she replied, and shuddered. 'Bbbrrrr, it's a cold one today.'

On her head she wore a hat with earflaps, mittens on her hands.

'And how is the hero doing, monitoring the schoolmistresses?'

'After a determined effort she realises that it's not the schoolmistresses who deviate from the rules but that it is she who doesn't understand the rules, and thus breaks them,' replied Álfrún Perla, and burrowed back into her reading. Ástríður Petra served tea. Ceremoniously we sat down on the grass.

Tea Party

'Did you see the egg?' Ástríður Petra said, and took a sip from her cup of tea.

'It's hard to miss,' I replied and sipped my tea, which burned my tongue.

'One of us finally managed to lay an egg and it was our bookworm, Álfrún Perla, who reads everything she can get her hands on – reading boosts fertility. But now nothing can go off course, the weather must improve,' she said and looked up at the sky: snowflakes fell from it. 'We'll invite you to the baptism,' she added as a flake landed on her eyebrow. I thanked her for the invitation. 'The swanling will be called Dimmalimm, or Prince, or Dimmalimmo.' Her attention alternated between me and the powder-white sky. 'Oh, you are so unhappy,' she added, 'how can we fetch you some happiness, Miss Humankind?'

'No, I'm not unhappy, quite the opposite. I am happy and fortunate,' I replied, going on the defensive.

'Ah, well, good to hear,' she replied and drank her tea, which was quite good – tasted like the broth of dandelion roots and winter blossoms, which I wasn't sure grew in this field. Ástríður said it was the most popular blend.

'That I can believe,' I said, and blew on the tea, warmed my hands on the cup, sipped it again and considered more closely the bright red mug, which was the same kind my grandmother had used to give me milk to drink at night. Then Ástríður Petra lunged toward me and took hold of my chin and forehead. The mug flew from my hands. She clamped my head between her palms and called for Álfrún, who slipped down from the heap with the distinct tranquility of a woman in a delicate condition. She sauntered closer, waving a pair of blacksmith's pincers.

'You shall feel for our toothlessness, Miss Privilegecunt – the toothlessness of the whole world,' said Ástríður Petra, holding me down. I fought against her grip until Álfrún Perla laid her entire bulk on top of me – and these creatures were no light-weights – shoved the pincers into my mouth, and pulled out a tooth. The blood spurted over all our faces and in the commotion I was able to get loose. Álfrún waved one of my canines in the jaws of the pincers. They laughed. My tongue searched for the hole while I wiped the blood from my glasses, spat and swallowed blood, tore a clump of grass from the ground and shoved it into the hole, stood up in my bloodied trench coat and pulled my bag toward me.

'Don't go,' they shrieked, 'don't go, our dear little Dionysia,' they screamed. Ástríður Petra rested the pincers against a tree. Álfrún Perla sat down on the egg and picked up her library book. I mattered less than I had thought.

DAYS OF CONSEQUENCE

7–11 April

At the Best Dentist's Office

In the bulletproof glass were sandblasted the words *Dental Repair, Oral Surgery*. My brother's best friend, Theodór, son of Linda and Máni, scuttled down the hall, stooped and splay-footed, and let me in. Silver hairs sprouted over the V-neck of his scrubs as he lifted the sunglasses from my nose. The skin is the most delicate soil, someone once said. I explained that I couldn't go to work with a missing tooth because of the ministries' requirements about appearance, that I had been attacked by militants who had invaded the stockroom, that the tooth must have fallen through a grate in the floor.

The official line – a cover story – was that we at the Special Unit worked in a stockroom and oversaw the acquisition of IT equipment for the ministries. That was why Teddi and Unnar sometimes came to me for advice about gadgets, and I had helped Teddi buy the 3D printer for his office. Shielded by white gloves, he drew out the bloody clump of grass from the hole in my mouth and scrupulously felt around the empty cavity. He had a canine tooth that would do for the time being, he promised. It would take some time to fashion a new one.

I followed my brother's best friend – he wore white foam clogs that snapped with every step, the quick marching rhythm of a slim man – into his workshop. There he offered me a whiff from a tin: early this morning he had pan-roasted and ground the beans to suit the day's humidity levels. Gerða, his wife, said his was the best coffee. Then he brewed some for us. We sat on stools that he had found in his father's garage and painted his mother's favourite colour, red. Máni and Linda never fought – we were sitting on *peace* stools. My brother Unnar believed his friend suffered from extreme nostalgia. Into a lily-white sink I spat blood tangled with blades and clumps of grass.

'Man, you really are something,' Teddi said and shook his head.

'I'm not a man, Teddi, even if I spit blood and other crap,' I replied.

Teddi had acquired the bad habit of calling me *man* after his other best friend passed away and he'd started inviting me on the camping trips they used to take to paint out in the wild. He fetched the temporary tooth from his safe, showed me to the chair in the next room, turned on a white radio, clipped a white bib around my neck, put a hose into my mouth that spewed soft water. Over a blue flame he warmed a canine tooth from the jaw of his deceased friend – who had bequeathed him his teeth in honor of their friendship – then stuck a pin into the hole and screwed the tooth onto the pin. The radio announcer declared that a department store looked forward to seeing us. That a petrol station was our best friend on the road. That nothing compares to the embrace of a jacuzzi. That some spare parts were the best. The announcements reminded me of my own false claims and empty promises.

At the end of the operation, Theodór admired his work: the tooth protruded, but it would have to do. He held up a mirror, which I pushed away. He refused to charge me. As we said goodbye, my brother's best friend wanted to give me a hug and I was in no position to insist that he hug instead the memory of his friend, the dead and generous gentleman.

The Parcel

Early the following Friday, Adda and Jónatan ushered me into the back room behind the security gate. I thought it was a joke. The air made me sneeze and I asked how many oranges they had eaten that morning. I also picked up the scent of drizzly mornings and antiquated pink billheads while contemplating a large clock hanging on a high, narrow wall. The clock's face was reminiscent of a pair of gaping jaws – spears piercing through the numbers (its teeth) 8 and 12. Jónatan rummaged in the blue-grey satchel with a powerful handheld scanner that the ministry had bought from Sweden early in the new year. A speck of dust was carried off on an undistinguishable ripple. I sneezed yet again and took off my trench coat at Adda's request. High on the wall the sun was fighting to pass through the thick windowpane.

'Four,' Adda replied and gestured for me to take off my sunglasses. Her eyes were forest brown.

'When did you open the first orange?'

'Seven on the dot,' Jónatan said and rummaged more thoroughly through the bag, which had many small pockets and compartments.

'Have you only eaten oranges today?' I asked, and lifted my arms, feet splayed.

'Also two eggs each,' said Adda, who traced a scanner around my arms, from my hips downward, up along the inseam and back down it, then up along the outer seam. She ran the device around my waist, felt with her fingers under the band, then scanned my torso along the front, the back, around the bra and my head, until around my cheek the device started screeching. It stopped after I screwed out the tooth. I sensed that Adda wanted to say that she had sympathy for those who lived with domestic abuse but was allowing only her face to express the sentiment.

'Thanks for not laughing,' I said.

'Why would I laugh?' she said, apparently surprised.

'Oh, one is often clumsy with words first thing in the morning. What are you looking for, anyway?'

'A routine random inspection,' Adda replied and handed me an orange.

'Routine?' I said. 'But it's never happened to me before.'

'Today we check every fifth employee, orders of the chief of police,' replied Jónatan, and he thanked me, said he truly – *truly*? – appreciated it, but since we weren't on personal terms I felt offended as he handed me my bag, his fists as big as boxing gloves.

I placed the orange on my desk and was about to hang up my coat when the unit's director of communications, Nói Ingason, grabbed my arm: I was expected in Selma Mjöll's office. Suspicions never sleep in a job like mine – what had I done wrong? The doors to her office stood open. Helgi Björn leaned against the bookshelf, held a stained coffee mug and fiddled with the copper scales with his little finger, wearing dress trousers, one foot crossed over the other, yellow socks, silver hair, a crisp white shirt. His closet housed a three-week supply of white shirts, Rósa had once informed Frankó in confidence. Selma rose from her seat in a new blue dress with a knight's collar, walked with a sly look on her face to the front of the desk, one foot in front of the other, and hugged me – something she never did, as I despised hugs. With a swift sisterly motion she hooked her arm under mine and pulled me out of the office.

'Early this morning a parcel arrived addressed to you. The explosives experts have vouched for its contents,' she said, and looked at the new old canine while I observed the makeup around her eyes. A fresh shampoo scent wafted my way. I wondered whether it would be possible to ban passengers on public transport from using scents and perfumes, especially in the morning hours, to avoid involuntary stimulation of the senses in public spaces. Axel,

Kristinn Logi,

Lóa,

Magnea,

Nói

and Úrsúla followed us into the kitchenette. Helgi Björn, also known as Venus – the alias Frankó and Rósa had given him, with his consent, to distinguish between work and play, and by way of disguise – brought up the rear. A large package on the table was addressed to:

Mme Elísabet Eva Unnar- and Rúnarsdóttir
Computers and Electronics, 3rd floor
Ministry of the Interior
13 Beam Street
City of R—, 313

But just as I was about to open the package with scissors, my canine came loose from its socket and landed with a clink on the wine-red floor.

'What was that?' said Magnea, whose powers of observation were exceptionally sharp.

This time I decided I had a right to the sanctity of a private life, and so fished the tooth quickly up off the floor and snuck it back into the cavity. Selma Mjöll snatched the scissors from my hands, her new soles skidding on the linoleum.

'Elísabet, whose birthday is 24 October, receives a gift on 8 April,' she said, and tore the wrappings off an egg similar to the one I had seen in the glade, tended by the bookswan Álfrún Perla.

Speckled, furry.

'It's larger than the egg of a shark, or an ostrich,' declared Lóa, wearing a pink kilt, her hair in a ponytail.

Úrsúla, wearing yellow overalls, touched the egg, and Kristinn Logi knocked on it.

'Seems real,' he said, wearing a striped Breton shirt and leather breeches.

Axel, who wore a light blue suit – he was, by his own account, having announced it often, trying out his bridegroom

finery, since he and Lóa were getting married this summer – urged them to take care: 'The egg could break and there
could be bacteria. Please use gloves.'

He went over the security protocols for the third floor. Our
bosses crossed their arms: Selma in her new dress and the
shoes with the brocaded pearls. Diamond teardrop cufflinks,
which Rósa had given Venus for his birthday, glimmered on
Helgi Björn's wrists. He asked me if I could explain the delivery
while Lóa and Magnea observed his delicate paunch and wide-
set hips.

'I should think so,' I replied, and removed my sunglasses
and the canine, which I showed them. I invited them all to
have a seat around the table and proceeded to tell my colleagues
everything that had transpired since I first saw the swanfolk
on that ordinary Sunday evening about two weeks prior. That
in some supernatural way the creatures were at once mammal
and bird. Unfortunately I didn't have any photographs to share,
but as they might all recall I stopped taking pictures after the
incident on the platform in Paris, when Selma and I attended
a conference on domestic violence and on the train I unthink-
ingly took photos of two bodybuilders who proceeded to throw
me down onto the tracks as soon as we alighted. I sketched
an image of the swanfolk on a piece of paper and passed the
drawing along.

Nói said he celebrated the discovery of a new species in the
animal kingdom. No one could have imagined anything like
this, Magnea added, it turns out there is something new under
the sun after all. Kristinn Logi said the human imagination was

not as boundless as it liked to believe, that it was not capable of inventing flying beasts out of thin air – stories of winged creatures other than birds therefore *must* be based in fact. Cautiously and sincerely, Úrsúla asked our bosses about my psychological state.

'The latest scans taken this week show an uncompromised cerebral hemisphere,' Selma explained, and added that I had really distinguished myself in the latest evaluations. The spring was surely a sensitive time but according to the tests I had achieved a 75 per cent credibility rating. My rating had improved over the winter months, and I was currently hanging at the lower range of the employee average, but as we all knew, no one in the unit had a credibility rating over 85 per cent.

Selma smiled beautifully to me once she had finished the elucidation and my colleagues turned their attention to Magnea, who, dressed in a camouflage suit, suggested inviting the creatures to take up residence in the City Zoo. There they could play a role in the education and upbringing of children.

Kristinn Logi suggested turning the area into a nature reserve, fencing it off and charging an entry fee – following an ecological survey and medical evaluation of the creatures in quarantine, in case they carried novel pathogens.

'But couldn't tourists just as easily bring new diseases into the country?' asked Úrsúla, who was a member of a lobby group for the construction of an international airport on an island out in the bay, where doctors in hazmat suits would sort travellers and refugees into groups based on physical strength and income. She had sent the Ministry of Foreign Affairs and the Ministry of Health recommendations for the design of the suits. Helgi Björn suggested we limit the discussion to the matter at hand.

'Yes and they speak our language,' said Lóa, and stuck a pencil into one of her dimples.

'And know how to write,' shouted Nói. 'Isn't it a global news story if animals can write?'

'But they aren't just animals,' Magnea reminded us. 'Up top the creatures are our sisters and brothers.'

Úrsúla asked whether I had posted the package myself. No, and as far as I knew I didn't walk in my sleep.

'Do you think the beings are connected to international gangs?' Kristinn asked. 'That they are meant to distract us while more serious crimes are committed in the country?'

Questions flooded the table while Helgi Björn poured coffee and served pink pastries from a wicker basket: How long had the creatures lived by the water? How had they travelled to the country? How had they learned the language? Had I noticed any phones or radios in the area?

No, I answered, and figured that the swanfolk had probably found the library book in a bin.

'Who on earth throws a library book in a bin?' Magnea said, indignant.

'Probably a pedestrian who lacks a feeling of collective responsibility,' answered Kristinn Logi.

Lóa raised her hand. She had just remembered a certain library book, *The Schoolmistresses in the City by the Bay* – she oversaw the annual assessment of books and read synopses of all newly published titles, assembled by the director of the state's book inventory, Natan Laufeyjarson, up on the fifth floor. She couldn't remember what this one was about, only that it had kept a low profile on the market, didn't sell at all, the author had left the country.

On the fifth floor of the ministry there operated a secret committee of seven readers who read everything published in print and online in the country. The eighth member, Natan, acted as their chairperson. I had once run into them in the hallway, though their departmental protocol forbade them from congregating as a group outside their workspace, a green room that Lóa had visited a few times, escorted by Natan. There the readers sat eight hours a day at seven desks under seven golden lamps. They subsisted on Italian coffee, French chocolate, Portuguese almonds. Off an inner hallway with a coatrack and hooks made of copper you could walk into a bathroom with seven urinals made of hand-painted Danish porcelain. In the workspace there lived three cats. The readers walked around wearing cowboy boots outdoors and felt slippers indoors, Lóa had told me, and she had seen them dancing with their favourite books at the committee's annual celebration. They were always dressed in light grey suits, with the same gentleman's haircut, similar gait. They looked guiltily at me when I ran into them in the hallway. It appeared to me that one of them had been crying.

From a Lost Text

Nói addressed the group: As a teenager he had read a book about prehistoric times, when goddesses and gods walked the earth alongside other animals – mostly invisibly, but not always. When our ancestors began making tools, the gods felt their work was done and left to experiment with life on other planets. But the goddesses didn't trust humans with the earth or to look after themselves – their judgement was too easily corrupted, they would never be self-sufficient like other animals – and so the goddesses stayed behind and amused themselves by pairing people off and developing personalities and appearances.

Nói rubbed his eyes – his lids grey, his eyes black, cherry lips; he wore a navy-blue jacket and a yellow shirt finished with a red-check bow tie – and continued:

'The goddesses had various complexions, some in colours there was never time to develop in humans. In bags over their shoulders they carried medicines and pigments and stimulating lovedust that they sprinkled over people on favourable and sometimes unfavourable occasions. They helped people to know themselves. They orchestrated conception directly and indirectly as they pleased and assisted women with pregnancy and childbirth. In ancient times child mortality was rare, labour always went to plan. If the goddesses were displeased by the prospects of an intended pairing, they took measures to hinder the union – by undermining the schemes of families who arranged their children's marriages, or sowing doubt in people's hearts through their dreams: an incomprehensible inner conflict, since the influencer was of course invisible, or at least indiscernible.'

'Boy, I can relate to that,' Magnea sighed.

'Always that invisible obstacle,' Úrsúla sighed.

'The goddesses slipped into people's dreams and spun fateful webs. Before the advent of mechanical power they assisted with agriculture and even steered the winds and clouds and helped plan the first cities. But technological advances began to rival people's faith in their own intuition, and the work of the goddesses was trivialised. People stopped listening to their dreams and in turn the goddesses became imperilled by the human race, who seized for themselves all land and all space, including all the psychic space that had been available – the way an apartment is *available* – which became occupied by humanity. The goddesses fled the cities to the forests and eventually abandoned the planet once humans began encroaching on the forests, too.'

Nói loosened his bow tie and wrapped it around his finger.

'Had humankind followed the goddesses' guidance and bothered to learn the dream language they used to communicate with people, developments on Earth would have been different. But I can see why people wanted to be in charge of themselves. Paternalism doesn't help anyone in the long run, yet the goddesses' interventions were something more than paternalism. Whether they were just amusing themselves or whether they could really see into people, that remains a mystery –'

'But where did the goddesses go?' asked Magnea.

'To other planets, and many of them were exterminated,' Nói replied.

'How could they have been exterminated if they were immortal?' Lóa asked.

'Their domain was usurped. They lived in dimensions that humankind commandeered,' Nói replied, undoing the top button on his yellow shirt.

'I don't understand,' someone said.

'If the ocean dries up, the fish die – if all land is submerged in the sea, the land animals die. The land of the goddesses – the psychic domain – disappeared under a flood of humanity, or a flood of human culture. Each person can easily eradicate from their mind, by filling it, the psychic space that ought to be kept free for spiritual reflection and meditation, dreams, epiphanies, and changes and influences to one's mentality.'

Indirectly, and most likely accidentally, Nói spoke contrary to our procedures at the unit, since we were sometimes forced in interrogations to breach the minds of our suspects, disconnect their faculties, and clutter their consciousness with frivolous trash in order to confuse it and extract the goods.

Magnea took the floor.

When she was a kid she had read a book about winged dinosaurs that were able to fly between continents, and even flew shorter distances with people strapped to their backs. During a world war all the winged steeds were exterminated, down to the very last one.

'Could have been reading the same book as me,' Nói said and buttoned his top button, fastened his bow tie around his collar. 'Strange that I don't remember the world war or the flying dinosaurs.'

'But how could such small people kill such enormous dinosaurs?' Axel asked.

'People don't lack imagination when it comes to exterminating species,' Kristinn Logi began, and sighed. 'They conspire so that the enemy, who don't know they're the enemy, voluntarily make their way to their own execution, sincerely believing the path to be favourable and of good fortune, well and truly believing they are headed for a celebration that will benefit both them and the world. When suddenly they find themselves caught in a deadly trap,' he added resentfully, as if we were the murderers. 'The winged beasts will have gone voluntarily into the snare while the humans sat around drinking and eating and debating love, the limits of existence, the beauty of the sea, and the free state.'

'Like how the cells of the body remember each bruise,' Nói continued and closed his eyes, his eyelids quivering to the rhythm of his vocal cords. 'The goddesses never forgot anything – *anything*. They didn't possess the power to forget, and their devotion was absolute. The burden of memory grew constantly heavier, they were exhausted by the weight of their memories, lamented the wickedness of man and became inconsolably sad, disappeared from civilisation and never recovered, because they could never forget. Some killed themselves. Which, if one is immortal, requires innumerable daring and horrific attempts.'

Kristinn Logi brought Nói a fresh glass of water.

The Special Unit was a great workplace and the good team spirit and work morale was all thanks to Selma's judgement of character and Helgi's talent for organisation. Helgi was more reserved than Selma at close range but spoke for the unit externally, attended meetings with the police, ministers and the security council, as well as other authorities, while Selma presided over the unit's internal affairs.

The egg lay in the centre of the table, proof that I couldn't have been lying, unless I had sent the egg to myself. We discussed whether the swanfolk could possibly belong to a species of goddesses who had been left behind on Earth, or one of the species nearly wiped out in antiquity. Helgi reminded us that Magnea and Nói had read books, not watched a documentary.

'What about that thing called human desire?' Axel interjected and waved his hands, which Lóa followed with her eyes, the movements of her head birdlike, like her ponytail. 'Man's desire to fly, man's desire to be a horse, to balloon to gigantic proportions or shrink to the size of a thimble – does everything need to be accurate and true?'

'A woman's desire to swim naked with a tail in the depths of the sea and listen to the whales' greatest hits?' Lóa asked.

Someone laughed.

Selma divided the employees into groups. One team would be in charge of carrying out a meticulous analysis of the egg – were it a bona fide egg it would require suitable conditions in order to hatch. Another team would search the area around the lake, look for signs of the creatures or the creatures themselves. I was to keep to the office, finish my report on the comics and lead a team that would investigate the library book and its author. Selma advised me to take my personal walks somewhere other than the green lake while the investigation was ongoing, unless accompanied by my colleagues and equipped with hardware that could capture evidence of the swanfolk and prove their existence. Selma's plan deprived my walks to the water of their futility and leisurely pretext. But she offered, perhaps as an attempt at compensation that I did *not* need, to accompany me on walks elsewhere, since a daily walk was essential for my mental health, that's what she'd heard – how I must have blathered on about myself on coffee breaks – and she, too, needed to get out after a long winter spent indoors. The ministry would pay for my dental repairs. Magnea and Nói were to track down the books they had read as children, but to cut a long story short they were nowhere to be found. The best-read people in the country, the team of seven on the fifth floor, and their aforementioned chairman, the head of the country's book inventory, Natan Laufeyjarson, had never heard of the work, or works. This conclusion did not bolster our faith in Magnea's and Nói's imaginations, since none of us was born yesterday, but rather strengthened our suspicions that the book, or books, had not only been remaindered and removed from the country's book-shelves and libraries, but had also been wiped from people's memories. According to the cognitive tests that employees of the unit undertook every quarter, Magnea and Nói possessed astonishing and unusual powers of memory, as well as a certain immunity to the zeitgeist – qualities in which lay their value to the unit.

By the end of the meeting I felt no respite, even though I had been told numerous times by psychologists and psychiatrists, and by nonspecialists alike, that on the heels of truth come liberation and relief.

At Rainbow Pizza

At the end of a monumental Friday, Selma Mjöll was determined to join me on my walk – she needed some fresh air – and Nói followed us down the stairs from the third floor, not shutting up about the obstinate winter, the docile spring, the weather's erratic shifts. Adda and Jónatan were still on duty at the gate, and as we approached they hid a pamphlet under the table. Selma walked briskly toward them. The clicking of her shoes echoed around the lobby and her coat trailed behind her like a red carpet. She grabbed the pamphlet, laid it on the table and said that of course they could look at pamphlets on baby carriages while they were at work. Their daughter, Sóley, was expecting. Congratulations rained over them. While putting on her red gloves, Selma said that subordinates ought to feel good at work, they didn't need to hide anything from her. The couple bowed. It would have been brusque of me to ask about the quantity of oranges and eggs they had eaten that day, or the Danish pastries served with the afternoon's coffee.

'I eagerly await the arrival of the leaf buds and the first golden plover. The moment I wake up I look out – a beautiful birch tree stands outside my window,' Nói said and wrapped a chequered scarf around his neck. In the outdoor light his face became tangible, his moles embossed, his wine-red hair palpable.

We came to a halt on the brick pavement in front of the building and looked to the sky, breathed in the glorious weather – neither cold nor warm, neither sunshine nor rain, the clouds like tufts of wool.

'You're impatient,' replied Selma. 'Have the cherry trees even blossomed abroad?'

'I don't know, but the golden plover is at least *supposed* to be in the country by now, according to custom,' Nói replied.

The arrival of the golden plover to the country's eastern shores heralded the formal beginning of spring – but at that moment my heartbeat quickened as I caught a whiff of a stirring in the earth, though there were no flower beds or trees in sight, only a fountain that had yet to be emptied of sand and which had never been connected to water. I asked them whether they could also smell movement in the ground, the worms stretching.

'Thank goodness for the mother tongue, otherwise we'd just be standing here stiffly staring into space – how awkward that would be,' Nói said and crossed his arms, his hands clad in enormous gloves.

'Agreed,' replied Selma, who was starting to grow uneasy. We said goodbye to Nói and strode off, me in my taupe trench and yellow knitted hat, Selma bareheaded in her red coat. A thick lock of hair fell over her face. She hooked my arm, leaned into me, stuck her hand in my pocket.

'You're the best,' she said.

'What do you mean, Rósa?' I asked, astonished.

'Just – you're the best, Beth.'

'You too,' I said out of politeness.

We threaded the city's waterline, the sea neither ruffled nor smooth. It was nearly dinnertime and we had arrived at a garage adorned with rainbow-coloured fairy lights that spelled out the establishment's name, draped like a necklace over the roof:

Rainbow Pizza

We sat down in a booth at the very back of the empty restaurant. From there we had a view over the whole place, as well as a bolt-hole if it came to a shoot-out. The window faced the car park outside. American country music played softly and mingled with the smell of basil, flour, tomatoes, the twilight and candlelight. The bandages around the waiter's index finger didn't bother him as he lit a white candle in a candlestick on the table and wrote down our order on a notepad.

'Anchovy pizza,' Selma and I said in a chorus forged by a love of anchovies.

The waiter disappeared behind a door but a little girl about eleven or twelve years old sat behind the counter, coloured in a colouring book and watched us – we stared at her: Should we stick earplugs in her ears? Ah, let's not worry about it, kids should sometimes be allowed to hear everything.

Still, I couldn't be bothered with any of this. Couldn't be bothered to act carefree and unencumbered, friendly, unfriendly, like a good employee or an average one, an inferior, a friend. Couldn't be bothered with the chitchat that came with it all, neither to speak nor to listen, but I knew I would none-theless listen well, talk a lot. The job required active listening, which in our free time became a habit. Selma scribbled insect-like with her fingernails on the back of my hand.

'Oh, Beth, it's been terribly, terribly hard,' she whispered and leaned over the table, straightened back up, her mother's wedding band glittering on her ring finger, looked at the girl, looked at me – *serious, intent* – hung her head, leaned over the table, scribbled on the back of my hand.

'I think I'm with child. Venus is of course the father. I am less excited about my first than he is about his seventh. I don't love him, but I don't hate him either, I care an awful lot about him and would rather not tarnish his reputation with an illegitimate child, nor ruin his and Dóra's happy marriage. Venus is a family man. I'm not a troublemaker by nature. I care about Dóra, Dóra is a *terrific* woman.'

Words emerge from the deep like a train from a tunnel, I read somewhere.

'We always take good long pauses in between, and in the interim I don't feel guilty of committing adultery. Each person is punished in their way. The day of reckoning is coming. I des-pise the word *homewrecker*.'

I started cleaning my sunglasses with a red handkerchief. The girl held a red crayon and scratched her head, pretended not to be staring at us, scratched her head even more.

'Having a child is certainly an investment,' I began, trying to hold up my end of the conversation, 'but the start-up cost

is considerable. I suspect Venus would want to help with that.'
I unscrewed my canine, which would be a hindrance were my
speech to be long. 'That is, until the child can pay its parents or
guardians back,' I added, though I knew little about the subject,
despite a number of the unit's cases having directly or indirectly involved the custody of children. 'Children are emotionally taxing, their upbringing draining, it takes a great deal of
time to raise one single child and to care for it – do you think
our parents would still be alive if they hadn't had us? I'm not
so sure, Rósa. Children bring happiness to the elderly. But the
cheapest option is probably abortion, in which case you'd break
even – notwithstanding the toll that it takes on the body, and
the intangible and incalculable losses in terms of expectation
and anticipation. But then again, the child might plunge you
into irreversible misfortune and financial difficulty. And pregnancy for nine months also drags the body down, even if it
does possess a remarkable capacity for regeneration. Yes, with
abortion you would be deprived of a potential investment that
otherwise would not be available to you unless you adopted
a child or got together with someone who was already a par-
ent. In order to have someone to talk to in old age. Time flies,
Grandma used to say. It's impossible to stop it. But children are
the future. Children will save the world.'

I used the candlelight to see if the lenses in my sunglasses
could do with more cleaning, and added: 'Do you suppose the
goddesses of fertility strapped the goddesses of frugality to a
chair while Rósa and Venus made love?'

'They fight over my body,' Rósa said.

'With the dutiful help of the goddesses of pleasure – were the two of you drunk?'

'One or two glasses of white wine.'

'Ouf. Do you think Dionysus would be granted legal domicile if they wanted to settle here?' I thought of the stateless swanfolk by the water, screwed in my tooth.

'What were you saying?' asked Selma, who didn't seem in the mood to hear anything new.

'Nothing,' I replied.

'I probably didn't orgasm, I can't remember. A mutual orgasm ought to be a requirement for conception. A minimum requirement. Oh, it's so good to talk to someone,' she added, distracted. 'What about you, Frankó, what's new with you? Do you still have that scrape on your ear –'.

The girl coloured even harder with her red crayon. What needed so desperately to become red? A castle? I cupped my ear.

'Oh just . . . I can't remember, nothing except that stuff with the swanfolk, which I told everyone about at length in the kitchen this morning,' I said. 'Yes, it's probably the most honourable thing to go to a clinic.'

'Mm, I see,' she said, and she grabbed my hand: 'You'll tell no one – it's just I can't remember when I last had my period.' She drew a deep breath and I drew one just the same.

'You got your period eight weeks ago.'

The waiter arrived with our pizzas.

'This is the best anchovy pizza around,' Selma said.

'Bon appétit,' the waiter replied and bowed.

Selma made eight radial cuts into her pizza, took and sent a picture of it. I knew to whom. Probably one could consider it an honour for an underling to know the secrets of her superior. In my childishness I deemed myself to have – in these selfish times – done a good deed by lending an ear to the troubles of a fellow citizen, and prouder than usual I cut myself a slice.

Over the Line(s)

As I cut myself a slice, basking in my own benevolence, I swelled with hubris and delivered, impromptu, the following speech:

'Rósa, or should I say my dear Rósa, though sometimes *my dear* sounds arrogant when it isn't meant to, and of course you aren't mine and I'm not yours. Please consider my support a given in each decision you make. I trust you to make the best choice for yourself, your relationship with Venus, and us at the Special Unit. The strength of your spirit throws the word *homewrecker* to the dogs. Don't worry about public opinion. That can be controlled through its outposts. You and I know that better than anyone. Pregnancy and childbirth wouldn't slow Venus down the same way it would you. I don't necessarily doubt that he sees the pregnancy as an opportunity to take over the unit. I read in an article online that it takes a whole village to raise a child, and I hope I will not shy from my duty as a villager.'

'Thanks, Frankó, it's good to hear that. You've never come out so unequivocally in favour of my love life, though I suspected I had your respect and confidence,' replied Rósa, and bit into a slice of pizza.

'The greater the sinner, the greater the saint,' I replied, and slapped my face with a knife.

'Oh, come now, don't judge yourself so harshly.'

'The greater the sinner, the greater the saint,' I repeated and slapped myself with the knife on my other cheek, started laughing hysterically. Selma furrowed her brow.

'Are you all right?' she said once I had regained control of myself and apologised for my behaviour. 'Are you seeing the psychologist regularly?'

My mouth closed, opened, closed, opened: *like a – like a – like a – like a . . .* garage door!

'Yes, and a psychiatrist at the unit every month,' I said.

'Good,' she replied, and how I despised her reply. *Good*. So say the powerful and the insincere. Go shit in your hat, I added in my head, but in that moment was forced to calm myself so I wouldn't start throwing furniture around in an innocent establishment – I grabbed hold of myself, focussed on the girl huddled over her drawing, who coloured more and more zealously with the red crayon, more zealously – I implored my heart, my heart, my heart, along with my inner strength, inner strength, begged them for composure. Surely my siblings wouldn't want their sister to lose her mind or plunge into ruin at a pizza parlour. And the girl looked up and into my eyes. The moment *answered my prayers*. I was able to get a grip, stopped despising the world – the garage door opened, closed, opened, closed – silently I prayed: Dear – dear – dear – *d e a r* – world, world,

w o r l d,

protect the girl with the red crayon like the cosmic egg itself.

And I was going and going, and really going, really, really,

really going to start to hate myself for the insincerities that my mind did and didn't tire of echoing, but Selma said:

'Representatives from the national security council met recently in the Tower . . .'

The Tower was a glamorous new gilded skyscraper in the city centre that I had never had the honour of stepping foot in. The view, I had read, stretched beyond the city to the ring of mountains to the east and across the bay all the way home to the sunset. Few had seen more wondrous sights than when in the evening light the seagulls reflected in the Tower's topmost windows, boats sailed from the harbour, and the sun set 'like a girl sticking her head underwater in the bathtub . . .' I had read that description while working on a certain project and subsequently written a report on the average citizen's interpretation of scenes in the city landscape.

For a time, a team from the Special Unit monitored a security guard named Jóakim Reynir who worked in the Tower but was later fired after a short story of his was published in a well-known literary magazine. The story was about the gulls that soared around the Tower in the twilight and which the night guards were tasked with exterminating, with poison and discretion, were there too many, so the story said. But the guards broke the rules, raised the gulls and named them, and at the end of the world, which the story described, the gulls took control of the country and made the security guards their ministers. From the highest ledge of the Tower the new rulers issued orders, which the ministers interpreted and broadcast over the nation through megaphones.

'You've got to be careful, Elísabet, especially now. It came up at the meeting of the council that it's about time for a promotion. You are a valuable employee of the Special Unit –'

'Don't,' I said and raised my hand like a traffic cop. 'A promotion would only mean a subsequent fall, which I would never be able to bear.'

'My dear friend, you can't constantly shield yourself from responsibility like a child. Just think what it's like to be me. Responsibility is deliberately thrust upon me. Someone has to take it, the baton can't just be passed around in endless circles. Right?'

How I wish I could explain how Selma pronounced the word *child*. I looked out the window and imagined that the rain falling in patterns on the glass was the excrement of birds. Certainly the birds understood the world better than I, who despised the words *certainly*, *moreover*, *furthermore*, *undivided*, *fatherland*, *good man*, *expediency*, *healthy relations*, *in due course*, *substantial*, *considerable* – these words and others offended my sense of modesty, my aesthetic taste, my entire worldview, which they took part in demolishing.

'The reward of the world is ungratefulness,' I said and yawned, and then Selma yawned.

You don't need to yawn just because I yawn, I would never have said, and I looked forward to getting home and taking a bath. I put on my sunglasses. We ate the world's best anchovy pizza.

Rósa and Frankó

In the red castle, which continued beyond the edges of the paper, a girl sat on a red chair in a red dress and spoke on a red telephone. Contented with pizza and dessert – chocolate cake decorated with yellow marzipan full stops and semicolons – we said goodbye to the waiter and the girl, who looked up at us haughtily. I nodded to her, a gesture that was meant to signify gratitude. The rain outside turned cold. I had left my yellow woollen hat in the restaurant but couldn't be bothered to run back. Rósa hooked her arm through mine.

'Despite everything, Frankó, I'm looking forward, when Venus and I are old, to knowing whether he still warms up at the thought of me.'

'Mm,' I said, 'definitely something to look forward to.'

'What do you really think?'

'He'll never stop,' Frankó replied. 'And maybe Rósa won't either.'

'I don't know about Rósa,' she replied, expectant and happy, 'but doesn't one have to hope? I've never made much use of hope, always prepared myself for the worst.'

'Yeah,' I replied, 'hope is nice.'

'Isn't it?'

'Yeah, I think so, but I'm not sure.'

'Oh, Frankó,' said Rósa and leaned up against me like a person on an album cover. Behind the rain the moon sucked its thumb. The writers' manual both encourages and warns against the use of metaphor, for it reveals simultaneously the author's insecurity and self-assurance. I despise it. I rely on it like a crutch in the text because of my self-loathing.

On our way home down the long streets – not a single car went past, nor a person, cat, gull, mouse, or rat, the lights from the streetlamps seemed to sparkle with an inner cold and insecurity – we were silent and to my mind I carried the particular responsibility that comes with walking alongside a pregnant woman: I was at the ready were she to fall or slip. The pavements remained icy in places. I would have accompanied Rósa anywhere and in any weather, day or night. Though she wasn't carrying any extra weight, by the time I got home my arm, on which she had rested her hand, was exhausted. Had I tried to play chess, I wouldn't have been able to move the pawns.

I hung my coat in the bathroom, wrapped cold compresses around my arm, listened to stand-up comedy on the web. So ended an evening that I never had any hope would come to anything. On a hang glider the night sailed in for a private audience, in through the doors leading to the back garden, dismounted in the living room with a soporific syringe like a quick-fire rifle in its arms, came closer, closer, I recoiled, it came closer, I recoiled, it jumped on me and pierced me and paralysed my organs – allowed me sleep, even though I had only ever brought the world harm.

How the night was good, and better than I.

'Thank you, night,' I whispered and wrapped myself in the duvet, imagined that I hung lifeless in a net made of spider's silk.

Sacred Gathering

M y superiors' designs and directives for me to stay within the city limits during the ongoing investigation into the egg and the events by the lake, unless accompanied and out-fitted with a wire, drove me up the wall. That Sunday my colleagues and I planned to meet at Hótel Absalón, which served the finest weekend brunch in town. And how I looked forward to drinking mimosas and discussing goddesses and the end of times, a new topic of conversation in the office kitchenette. Balance is achieved in life only when one no longer knows whether one wakes or sleeps, I read somewhere. Saturday afternoon, in fair weather, I headed east towards the lake.

Had I betrayed the confidence of the swanfolk with my testimony in the kitchenette? But surely they had invited my revelation when they sent us the egg, however that had been achieved in practice. Confidentiality was the foundation of my profession. At work I was tasked with gaining the confidence of as many as my mind could bear.

On Saturdays there were more people running around the lake than on weekdays. The still weather also encouraged it, though it was cold. There were countless local running clubs who rallied their members on weekends, and the path around the green lake was a customary link in their route. I walked around the water and looked up the slope, then heard a whistle: a humanswan with a purple, avian lower half, wearing a red jumper, peeked out from behind a bountiful aspen. No one saw me as I jumped onto a mound, over some tussocks and behind a bush. She introduced herself: Fjóla – said she was an envoy.

'Fjóla?' I asked, by way of confirmation.

'Isn't it a beautiful name, Missis Elísabet Eva?'

'It is.'

We bounded up a steep hill overgrown with trees, descended on the opposite side, then went up another. Beyond it we came to a glade. There swanfolk sat in a circle and exclaimed when we appeared. I heard both giggling and roaring laughter. Fjóla crammed me into the circle. I was welcomed by those nearest to me with harsh patting and rough hugs. In the middle of the circle a creature lay facedown under my grandmother's blanket, but its face was obscured; only a yellow hood was visible, covering the back of its head. A red-haired cat was lying beside it. The leader sat opposite me on the pink cushions. Ástríður Petra sat beside her.

'Welcome, Missis Elísabet Eva, daughter of Unnur and Rúnar. Nice to see you again. Thank you for daring to come back here despite everything and everything and everything,' the leader shouted and lifted a jar filled with clear liquid.

Ástríður Petra also lifted a jar: 'You know, Elísabet, we knew you'd come back. You just can't leave us alone. Are you obsessed with us? Be honest.'

She laughed and downed her drink.

'What are you looking for? Another scuffle? To lose your other canine? What is your business here, Missis Human?' asked the leader.

The squawking among the group suggested that they had no concerns about surveillance or coming under siege.

'Amiable leader,' I said, and tried to sound at once like a messenger from an allied troop and an impartial emissary from a rival battalion. I placed my palm against my cheek on the side where I had lost the tooth. 'Amiable Ástríður Petra, distinguished guests. I do not know the feeling of longing except through hearsay, have heard that it resembles a desirable stomach ache. But now I can almost assert, almost admit, to having experienced such a yearning despite everything and everything and all of it being altogether painless.'

Ástríður Petra and the leader burst out laughing.

'You're insane,' Ástríður replied. 'She's completely bonkers . . . you're a freak . . . she's . . .'

'A deranged ewe,' the leader concluded.

They stared at me for a long while – their eyes glazing over – I felt uneasy – didn't like the look of things – felt unprepared for what might come, what could happen and what couldn't happen and what shouldn't happen. I counted twelve beasts. The thirteenth was the one lying in the centre, who appeared to be sleeping.

'Did you get the parcel?' shouted the leader.

'Yes,' I yelled back, and the others who had been chattering in hushed tones grew quiet. 'The egg has arrived and is in a warm and safe place, you can all rest assured that it will receive the best care an egg can get.'

'Cheers to our egg,' the leader shouted. 'May our nestling flourish and thrive in the world of man like the most darling showpiece.'

'Cheers!' everyone shouted, then clinked and downed their glasses.

'The egg is the rent we pay to the city in the hopes of continued cohabitation and cooperation,' the leader explained. 'With it we also buy ourselves time to think while we choose the lesser of two evils.'

'But why pay rent if no one's charging?' I said.

'It's a down payment. The egg is our hope for a future for our species here on Earth,' the leader said. 'We held a referendum and this was the result: to send the authorities an egg. Do you realize, Miss Human, that our survival depends on the mercy of others?'

'At your service,' I said.

'Did you tell them everything you know?' Ástríður Petra said.

'Not everything, only that I had met a few swandames who lived by the green lake, that they were dying of cold, needed assistance from the authorities in bringing up their young, fostering them in the City Zoo.'

Soffía, who sat with a grey cat in her lap, invited me to try some worm wine. Lena then ladled some from a tub into a jar that was passed to me, before topping up everyone else.

'This is a milestone victory, a formidable milestone victory,' Ástríður Petra shouted, and chinked glasses with the leader.

Lena told me not to worry, that the drink contained none of the drugs that humans secretly slipped one another.

'You see, Miss Elísabet Eva, we don't claim to be better than you all, even though we don't spike your drinks. We would let you know first: 'Here you are, would the lady like a roofie?' That's the difference – see?'

I saw the difference.

'But we don't blame you humans or judge you even though you have different customs. Our traditions aren't morally superior or more sophisticated, though we would *never* slip one another drugs or other poisons. Were our population to number in the millions we might slip each other poisons, though it's impossible to know,' Lena said, and ladled from the tub into more jars.

'Yes, it's not as simple as saying that we are better because we don't poison one another,' Soffía agreed.

Blíng shook her fair locks, her eyelids a summer yellow: 'It's not as simple as knowing whether humans lie and tell the truth and poison one another for reasons other than the need to survive. Like how humans eat and sleep out of the need to survive. Does one lie because of this need? Does one tell the truth because of this self-same need – *to survive*? If I had to slip others poison in order to survive, would it be a justified act? *To survive*. We judge no one. Sorry if I sound confusing,' she added and rubbed her eyes, spreading out the sun-yellow colour on her eyelids.

María raised her hand emphatically:

'Hello – can you hear me? Hello! Can you hear me okay?'

'Yes,' answered a few, and most of the others fell silent. Soffía lit candles and passed them along. They stuck the candles into the ground in a circle around the creature who was lying in the centre.

'I know why humans tell the truth,' announced María and laughed.

'Why?' asked Kornlilja and wiggled her eyes. Kósetta and Mandý sat beside her, painting their nails.

'To spare their memory. Lying is more costly to the memory,' María said.

'For economic reasons,' concluded Soffía.

'For economic reasons,' echoed Blíng.

The level of inebriation in the group was substantial and beyond question.

'But why does one lie?' Kornlilja asked, weaving a wreath from young birch branches.

María: 'One *l i e e e e e e e e s . . .*'

She stretched the word like an accordion book, bought herself time, since countless possible answers awaited her: an answer that entertained; an answer that shocked, provoked.

Kornlilja took the floor and directed her words at me: 'The verb *to lie* is the most beautiful verb in your language. It sounds like a quiet adventure.'

Each one pronounced the verb *lie*, while others sang it.

'The verb *to fool*,' said Kósetta in a loud voice that overwhelmed the others, 'sounds like I'm licking chocolate icing off my finger: *fool . . . fool . . .*'

She pretended to lick her fingers, which shone with fresh nail polish.

Álfrún Perla, who sat farther away with Ástríður Petra and the leader, waved to me and shouted:

'Missypants, send all my worthless precious almighty love to the egg in the brooder box. Like a true expectant mother who, unfortunately, betrays her maternal instinct, I beg of you: if a land other than the City Zoo awaits the rest of us who sit here in this fair glade – perhaps a potter's field – then please, for a mother who betrays her nature, I beg you, take care of the egg and the treasure that grows inside it. Mummy says hello.'

Álfrún Perla sent countless finger kisses my way. Her lips stained her fingertips.

'The father-to-be of the hatchling in the egg, Earl Prince Karl, also sends his regards,' she added and blew a very long kiss, and for a second I thought I

s a w

a red butterfly

take off, fly out of the glade, and disappear. I was going to ask whether Earl Prince Karl had fertilised the egg, and I looked around for someone to whom that name might belong. In a dim corner sat a creature I didn't recognize. She had her hands folded on her lap.

Kornlilja turned to me again: 'It's a shame your language doesn't have a special verb for telling the truth, the way it has one for *to lie* and, for example, *to walk*: *I told my legs to move in the direction of home* instead of *I walked home*. The truth is compositional, not elemental. The verb *to truth*, as far as I know, doesn't exist in your language.'

'Language covers reality like a cloud – no, language covers

reality like a tent,' María said, or rather mumbled, one of her hands describing slow circles, 'and there's a hole in the tent where the simple verb *to tell the truth* should be, and it leaks in through the hole, which only means one thing: human reality *l e a k s.*'

She pointed suddenly with a forceful index finger: 'To tell the truth – *to truth* – is not natural to the language like *to love, to run, to eat, to speak*. The truth needs crutches. Long ago human beings mortally wounded the truth such that it will never recover! *Never!* The language reveals this weakness of mankind. The lie is strong and free, even if it traps the liar in all sorts of chains.'

María clapped for herself. It seemed to make no difference whether anyone had been listening. She lit a wad of dockweed, exhaled a cloud of smoke that obscured her face. It began to snow. The candle flames devoured the snowflakes, making faint, darting sounds like something shattering. A few of the swanhumans opened umbrellas and sheltered those who sat near.

Mandý scribbled with a yellow pencil in a notebook and asked: 'But what about the verb *to prove*?' I was curious to see what kind of alphabet she was using, and her handwriting. 'Surely that word doesn't need crutches?'

'The verb *to prove* dispels the lie with reason, and more often than not one proves oneself with lies,' replied Lena, who proceeded to rip up some grass and sprinkle it over the tub alongside the snowflakes, then stir the worm wine with a whittled branch.

Soffía furrowed her shapely brows and bit her lip: 'The word *fact* is reminiscent of a coffin,' she said softly, her lip bleeding, 'also of a glass jar and dining room furniture. The word *falsehood*, however, is reminiscent of a swamp, tinned food, strangeness, a screech, wine, a rake, warmth, a field of berries.'

She listed the words slowly so Mandý could catalogue them.

I pictured two gardens and put Soffía's words about facts and falsehoods into them and considered whether the gate between the gardens stood open, closed, or locked.

Kornlilja looked up from her needlework and furrowed her brows just like Soffía furrowed her brows: 'But why a berry field, Soffía?'

Soffía smiled at Kornlilja.

'The truth is clear as a spring,' declared Lena and stirred the wine.

'The truth is spring,' Blíng sang, 'the lie is autumn.'

'The truth is a doorbell, a knock on a door,' Fjóla said.

'The truth is God!' shouted Mandý and waved her pencil. 'The lie is flattery.'

'The thrifty *never* lie, unlike the generous,' said Soffía, and dabbed the blood from her lips with the sleeve of her jumper.

María let her eyelids droop – heavy silver eyelids, long eyelashes – and lowered her voice: 'I would hold the truth in my arms like a newborn and let it drink from my breasts: Mm, little sick weak truthbaby, how mummy loves you and wants to empty her body for you.'

My eyes were drawn equally to everyone. Were I to look and listen to Kósetta I would fear missing out on seeing and listen-

ing to Lena, or Mandý, or Blíng, or Kornlilja, or Álfrún Perla, or
Soffía, or Fjóla. Each time María blew smoke, my burden light-
ened. More of them brought flames from the candles on sticks
and lit wads of dockweed, stuck the sticks into the ground.
The smoke from the burning leaves made me cough. I wet my
throat with the worm wine. Álfrún Perla took off a mitten and
measured the snowfall with her palm. Snowflakes freckled it as
she spoke.

'Elísabet Eva, listen up, here comes a riddle: Does Álfrún
Perla miss the egg or not? Can she miss something she will
never know?' She closed her hand and muttered, 'The answer
sleeps inside the riddle and refuses to wake up.'

I wanted to soften her temper, to ask the bookswan whether
she had finished reading the story about the schoolmistresses,
took down my sunglasses but couldn't manage to make eye
contact with her.

'There we have it,' María muttered and sipped her worm
wine. She hiccupped, then dried her lips with the red handkerchief.

'The lie is camouflage, the truth is nakedness,' Fjóla announced and wiped away the tears that trickled down her
cheek.

'May I?' said Kósetta, holding a brush. I gave her permission
to cover up my black eye with powder from a jar marked with
the initials of a Polish cosmetics manufacturer: *M.F.*

Ástríður Petra and the leader, who had been whispering to
each other, asked what was being discussed so fervently.

'Lies and truth – but we have exhausted the subject,' explained Lena as Kornlilja crowned Lena's head with a coronet of birch twigs, 'the floor is yours.'

Álfrún Perla blew her nose heartily, took off her hat, brushed and braided her hair, and said, speaking quickly: 'Once there was a fair and clever maiden who had two hands. One was called Truth, the other Falsehood. Happy and well, the maiden walked the whole of the world. Some days the right hand was in charge and some days the left. Some days neither was in charge, and on those days she wandered about aimlessly and let herself be pushed around. One day, she decided that one hand would take charge of the other. She wanted to simplify a life that had become too varied, too chaotic – she had met too many people, been entangled in too many good and bad things, had one too many times not known up from down. She decided to host a competition in order to decide which hand would take control, the right or the left. The competition went on for many days and ended with the maiden sitting at a table with an axe ready to chop off one of her hands, the losing hand.'

Álfrún Perla tied a ribbon to her braid and replaced her hat.

'And what happened? Which one won the competition?' Mandý said.

'Everyone is welcome to choose the fate that suits them,' replied Álfrún and handed her jar to Lena, who filled it from the tub.

'I would have chopped off my lying hand,' said Soffía, who was stroking the fur of the cat whose name, she said, was Greyman Jeepson.

'For me, the other hand,' said Kósetta, and grimaced when I declined the offer to see in a mirror how well she had concealed the purple eye. 'The truth is somehow always in everyone's and everything's way.'

'Were I the fair and clever maiden I would have chopped off my head,' said María.

'This is a boring story,' said Blíng, who was crocheting a yellow children's glove, 'kindly tell a different story about lies and truth.'

Soffía stroked Greyman as if she were strumming a guitar and said: 'Once, as so often, the lie put the truth to bed: sleep tight, fair and good truth, and rest well. The truth grew tired quicker than the lie and had more need of rest, slept better and deeper and longer, but the reasons for this were unknown, unless it's true what they say, that a clean conscience sleeps sounder than a tainted one – but that has long been debated and what do I know. Anyway, the truth fell asleep while the lie sang unbelievably beautiful lullabies and was finally itself about to fall asleep when it was alerted by a rustling and began to suspect thieves were afoot and so went and fetched its sword. It is my duty to protect the house of truth, the lie shouted and plunged its sword into three thieves – whose names were Duppy, Dopey, and Dazzle – and in so doing woke up the truth. *I killed the invading army,* she shouted with the sword aloft. And the truth replied, *Thank you for protecting my house, Mother dear, let us rest now.* The lie and the truth yawned and fell asleep in each other's arms.'

Greyman jumped out of Soffía's lap and disappeared. Lena shuddered: 'Soffía, where did you learn that horrible story?'

she said. 'Is the lie then the mother of the truth, and the truth the daughter of the lie?'

'Yes,' said Soffía.

'These are loathsome, repulsive family ties,' whispered Lena, hiding her face in her hands. 'I *cannot* take any more, I cannot *take* any more.'

Blíng demanded a different story about the parties in question.

'The truth was a locked glass chest and the lie was a hammer that men used to break the chest and spread the truth around the whole world,' said Kósetta, quick-spoken, 'then the hammer changed into a box of sweets that never runs out—'

Blíng sighed. She was none the wiser. María stroked her hair: 'My dear, it's hard to understand that which is constantly evolving,' she whispered.

'No thank you, none of that!' shouted Blíng. 'I *must* get to the bottom of this.'

'Me too!' shouted Mandý, holding her pencil aloft.

'Ask the representative of mankind at the party,' suggested the leader.

I discreetly tightened the tooth in my jaw, then sipped the wine, which was bitter, soft and thick.

'I am considered an authority on lies and truth,' I began my speech, 'and it is my job to conceal the truth with plumage and also with plucked feathers – it all depends on what is most appropriate to each game of hide-and-seek, which is to say: we put the truth in the appropriate costume, a fresh coat of feathers. I also work at gathering various truths in one place, into a kind of truth museum. The job of protecting the truth also requires archival and security services of some description, as some truths belong to private collections. There are laws in this country concerning property rights. I make sure people can't get close to truth X, and if people do get dangerously close to truth X it is my duty to chase the snoopers off.'

'So the truth is a glass chest guarded by dogs?' said María.

'Yes. However, we have many different types of truth. Humans have no say in the truth of the heavens and yet they work at pretending to know something about it. Every day the truth of one person collides with the truth of another in varyingly harsh and unexpected and unforgiving circumstances.'

I was grateful for the looks that fell upon me, a mix of wonder and approval. Lena ladled some wine from the tub and filled the jars, which were passed along. The liquid shimmered. Night had fallen, the snow had stopped; the moon shone high and full in the sky. The creature, who lay facedown under the blanket in the centre of the circle, did not move. Snow covered its yellow hood.

'But who sleeps there so soundly, may I ask?' I asked, and was about to dust the snow off the hood. The red-haired cat stood up, stretched, and yawned a long, languorous yawn, baring its sharp teeth.

'We are sorry to inform you of the passing of our beautiful and good brother,' said the leader. 'His name was Mikael, we called him Mikki. Our dear prince Mikki died of exposure. There was nothing we could do.'

'Or he might have eaten some of the poison that the

maintenance staff spread around the area to exterminate pests,' said Ástríður Petra, 'we don't know and we never will. He was sitting there under the poplar yesterday,' she added and pointed east, 'whittling cutlery for the wedding party. He and Móa . . .'

Móa was the one in the dark corner sitting with her hands in her lap, wearing a net over her face.

'. . . were due to be married. He had whittled three sets, one for each of the nestlings they hoped to have.'

Ástríður showed me the cutlery.

'They wanted to have cutlery at the banquet like at the weddings of humans.'

I touched the delicately carved objects made of young birch wood.

'Missis Elísabet, do we laugh too much while we mourn?' María said, then shoved a wad of dockweed with stone-dead embers into the ground. 'How do humans mourn? No one taught us any customs. Everyone died like we have told you too many times, because we are plagued by the inferiority complex of wretches that no one listens to, and so we repeat ourselves in the tireless hope that in the end our words will finally get through.'

I examined the soft, sculpted cutlery, wondered whether Mikael had been so well equipped as to have had access to sandpaper, with what tools he had whittled the pieces. The group awaited my answer. Lena repeated the question:

'Missis Elísabet, do we laugh too much at our brother's wake?'

'Maybe,' I replied reluctantly.

'And maybe not?' said Ástríður Petra.

I sensed her hostility had reawakened.

'Yes, and maybe not,' I replied.

'Tell us the truth like we would tell you the truth if the worm wine were spiked. Did you think earlier, "Strange how badly they behave at their brother's wake"?' María said.

'Yes, I thought that by accident,' I replied, presiding over my own trial.

'Thank you for telling the truth,' said María and sighed.

'It was my pleasure, so to speak,' I replied and touched the edge of the knife, which was both sharp and soft, hard and tender. Gently, I scraped myself.

'So to speak how?' someone said.

'She thought it *accidentally*,' someone repeated after me.

'Was that so hard? To tell the truth, *to truth*, when it came to it, Miss Elísabet Eva?' Lena said.

'You butter your fingers, that's for sure,' said the leader. 'You sit here unsure of yourself and try to conceal your vanity and humanity out of fear of having your jaw grabbed – of losing the other canine. Yet *still* you came here, even though you have absolutely everything to lose, and you fashion your answers to elicit the ideal reaction, which you quickly calculate that we will show.'

'Yes,' I replied and passed the cutlery along.

'Tell us: How do you humans conduct yourselves at the passing of your closest kin?' said the leader.

'We cry, stay quiet, cry more, remember . . .'

'*R e m e m b e r*,' replied the leader with awe.

'Do you want to know why we laugh and misbehave while

we hold vigil over our brother's remains?' said Álfrún Perla.

'No, maybe I don't want to know that,' I replied.

'Let's give her a round of applause, the humanfool answered in line with the truth!' shouted Álfrún Perla, and they clapped their hands and clinked glasses for the humanfool Elísabet Eva. Blíng adjusted the blanket covering Mikael.

'Our poor brother who died of cold,' she said in a hushed voice. 'Our brothers are more sensitive and cannot stand the cold as well as their sisters, and they can't distinguish as well between food and poison. My Órekur sleeps all hours under the fur coat I found and can't be bothered to wake, and when he does he grumbles something unintelligible. Poor Earl Prince Karl is missing but hopefully he'll sleep it off somewhere and wake up soon.'

She covered the corpse entirely with the blanket so no part could be seen. I was going to ask Blíng about Órekur and Earl Prince Karl but Soffía put her finger to her lips as a signal for me to keep quiet, and I kept quiet, like them, for so long that the silence threatened to drive me mad, until eventually they closed their eyes and sang in that unknown language. I enjoyed the sounds and strange chords. One of them opened her eyes and gestured to me to close mine. The leader cleared her throat and the singing stopped, then she spoke.

'As long as murders are committed in the name of nations, cultures, faiths and ideologies, and peoples, and living beings are forced to endure insurmountable hardships and are abandoned in their plight by those in charge of welfare, then no one has a right to private sorrow. A minister mourns his mother and the same day signs a document authorising the murder of someone else's mother – what is that?'

She waited, it seemed, for my answer, but I was busy wondering whether I had arrived at a meeting of a religious cult. Then I felt as if I had been slapped without being touched. The leader lifted her ski goggles and looked at me with a gaze that most would find dear.

'Say something in defence of your society,' said Ástríður Petra, and I lifted my jar:

'Cheers,' said the human delegate.

The creatures laughed or screeched, cheered – downed their drinks, then tipped out their jars into the grass. Lena closed the tub. Six or seven swandames stood up and carried their brother out of the clearing.

'Your presence is no longer desired,' said Ástríður Petra. 'We need to whittle more cutlery.'

Fjóla pulled me to my feet and offered to escort me to the water. I said I knew the way but the swanfolk insisted on the accompaniment. Fjóla went ahead of me and must have been able to see in the dark, she lifted the tree branches to ease my journey. 'Don't be afraid,' she whispered when we had almost arrived. I said that I had been trained in such a way that eliminated the fear response from my nervous system. She pretended to laugh, pushed her palms under my butt and I flew out of the dell, down to the lakeside path, landed on all fours, scraped my knees, my palms, my elbows.

The lampposts had been lit.

A group of people in reflective clothes ran west. Tourists in a

bus watched me clamber up the dusty gravel beside the highway. My phone rang. Rósa invited Frankó over to her yellow
sofa to watch a movie and eat popcorn. 'Thanks anyway,' I replied, and didn't attend the lunch at Hótel Absalón the next day
either. I was in as much need of rest as the truth on a good day
and felt I needed to sleep for days but instead awoke well-rested
at the right time on Monday morning and decided once and for
all – for the sake of my own interests and sanity, and in fealty to
myself – that I had dreamed a long and winding dream seemingly without end.

THE INVESTIGATION

~April 11–20

'No One Misses Themself' –
The Pincers & the Tooth

The team investigating the area around the green lake, searching for evidence of the swanfolk, found my tooth in a clearing that, according to their measurements, lay at a distance of 700 steps from the path. I didn't recognise the clearing, but to cut a long story short the tooth was sent to a laboratory where it was ascertained that a rare tool had been used in its extraction. Commercial registries revealed five pincers of the same make in four households in the country: three still in their original packaging and another in active use in a carpenter's workshop; the owner of the fifth, Axel X, was deceased. The man's heirs didn't recall a set of pincers among his estate, but said he had had a proclivity for the outdoors and had sketched water fountains in his spare time. They offered up his sketchbooks as evidence. There my colleagues and I came across drawings of fountains in cities across the world, as well as in imagined places, alongside descriptions of birds. The following paragraph rightly caught our attention:

Last night I met a new lover who is not of this world.
Though we have no grounds to understand each other,
we understood each other. Our parting was pleasant, not
painful or fraught and uncomfortable like partings between
lovers are wont to be. My lover simply said: What will be
will be. If I understood him correctly. Then I walked to my
bike. The sun was setting as I opened the lock, and when I
looked back he rose up like a chieftain from the reeds and
waved. I envied his view. This evening I was so cold that I
shivered so I took an anti-inflammatory – 1 g of Tylenol,
followed by 500 mg of Vicodin – and subsequently couldn't
go to work because of a chill and a general malaise. I feel
strange but I don't miss him. No one misses themself.

His heirs didn't mention, and this omission we considered reprehensible, that during his lifetime the man had been convicted of rape. After having admired his journal writings, we were particularly upset by this news. A few of my colleagues went to the rapist's grave armed with silenced pistols and emptied a few rounds into his plot, drank whisky, smoked cigars, then headed to a nearby sweat lodge to purge themselves of evil spirits.

No signs of the swanfolk were found in a fine-tooth comb search of the area around the lake. Many specimens were taken of things that turned out to trace back to men, children, horses, dogs, rabbits, cats, sheep, mink, mice, foxes, rats and swine. The bins were searched and samples taken from the water, but all specimens had sources in previously known and documented collections. The staff of the municipal building installed security cameras in carefully selected locations based on my instructions. Nothing unusual was captured on the video. A few times a person walked through a clearing, people met, made love, ate packed lunches, drew pictures of trees, answered calls of nature, drank from thermos flasks; a dog ran over a hill and a person followed, cats roamed about; there were mice and foxes, familiar species from bird registries, and industrious ravens gathering bric-a-brac into nests.

Sign-off

That week I requested yet another extension for my report about stand-up in the city. I was granted the extension and in turn gave Selma permission to read the latest draft. Then I took my scratched tooth and the referral from the ministry to Teddi, who made us the best coffee from his home-roasted beans. We sat down on Linda and Máni's peace stools and their son showed me a new painting of his wife and his deceased friend sitting together by a fire in front of a yellow tent in a wonderful wine-red evening landscape. They had never met, his wife and his late friend – the men had always gone alone on their camping trips to paint landscapes. Now Teddi was able to unite his two favourite people in a painting. We flipped through an album of photographs from their camping trips. The married couple would go on city trips abroad instead. Just then I pictured the husband and wife in light-toned linen clothes, chained down to airplane seats, eating food off trays, with handcuffs loose enough that they could move their hands and the cutlery, with which it was impossible to harm oneself. When they finished the meal their mouths wouldn't need to be taped over like with some people, because they belonged to the class of manageable passengers. In this train of thought I suggested to Teddi that he paint his wife and his deceased friend on a prison transport flight, wearing orange prison garb and shackled to their seats – unaware that artists hate it when people suggest subjects for their works. Theodór leafed carefully through the album so its silk pages crinkled and said that he found the idea disgusting.

'What about painting a picture of your wife breastfeeding?' I said stubbornly, trying to regain his good graces.

'Done it, have about fifty paintings of Gerða breastfeeding the kids,' Teddi said. I pretended to want to see the paintings. He didn't reply.

'Tell me about your wife,' I said, eager to show a healthy and enlightened interest in humanity. He closed the album and shot me a sharp look:

'What for, Elísabet?'

'What kind of woman is your wife?' asked the little sister of his best friend, having shrivelled down with shame at having angered her brother's best friend. But I was also curious and excited to know whether his wife belonged to the category of *terrific women*.

'*She's a good woman*,' replied Theodór and laid down the album. 'This is not something I care to discuss, Elísabet.'

'Prison transport,' he repeated when I was lying in the chair with a hose hanging on my lower lip, spouting tepid-soft water into my mouth. He removed his best friend's canine from my mouth and put mine in its place. The other went back into the chest with its sister teeth and from there into the safe.

'Thank you, Theodór,' I said, and we settled the bill. 'I look forward to laughing in the kitchenette without having to cover my mouth. And not having to screw it out if I want to speak at length. This one sits stock-still,' I added in a robotic tone.

We didn't hug or kiss as we said goodbye, and I was relieved. The paved square outside the building with its innumerable white-painted and windowless passageways and stairwells was made from 360,390 love letters that had gone through a shredder and been blended with milk and rubble from the mountains.

The Diamond Reserve

The library book that the bookswan Álfrún Perla had been reading in her quarters, *The Schoolmistresses in the City by the Bay* by Úlfur Högnason, features a character named Issa Blóðberg whose job it is to monitor teaching methods in elementary and high schools in a small city by a purple bay. At a protest on Parliament Square, a group of schoolmistresses draws the attention of the organisation that Issa works for. In the hopes of getting closer to her subject she falls in with one of the teachers, Ella Marta Daníelsdóttir, by romantic means. The same evening that Issa files a report to her superiors providing evidence that the group intends to overthrow the patriarchy through propaganda, unorthodox teaching methods, and various major and minor acts of vandalism, Issa falls suddenly ill with food poisoning and is admitted to the hospital.

Following a period of drug-induced delirium – in A&E she is pumped full of painkillers whenever she asks for buttered toast with cheese, and the book describes her psychotropic journey to hell and back – she wakes up in a hospital bed in a psychiatric ward. When she walks into the hallway, dressed in generic hospital garb – long men's trousers and a loose-fitting nightshirt – she discovers the aforementioned school-mistresses stationed in the visitors' chairs beside the patients' beds. A part of their operation involved, it turns out, psychologically breaking down their romantic partners, thus exacting revenge for the emotional entrapment of women going back hundreds of centuries. Meanwhile, the guest chair beside Issa's hospital bed radiates a sad emptiness. On her bedside table lies a break-up letter from Ella Marta, which vanishes in Issa's hands while she reads it – at the same time she hears Ella's sinuous laughter and sees her walking down the hall supporting another patient, with romantic undertones.

By the end of the book Issa is disabused of all trust; she is destitute, her computer wiped, her phone taken away; homeless and jobless, she steps onto a stool in the hospital laundry and wraps an electric cord around her neck.

At the national library, Axel, Lóa, and I, the team tasked with investigating the library book, discovered that no copy of the book was missing from the collection. The librarians vouched that each and every copy stood whole in its place on the shelves. The book's lending records listed five readers. We contacted each of them and they remembered little of the plot; two had never started the book because of a lack of time, two hadn't finished it for the same reason, and the one who had read it, hurriedly, vaguely remembered a sad ending. The five of them swore to not having loaned the book to anyone else, or taken it on a walk out beyond the city. I swore that the copy the bookswan had in her possession, which I had handled, was authentic and bore the seal of the National Library. According to sales reports, seventy copies of the book had been sold. It was not deemed necessary to interrogate the buyers.

The team then gained access to a stockpile of copies due to be remaindered by the publisher. We promised to return them so they could be destroyed, since it was illegal to give away copies removed from sale. We distributed the book among our colleagues, who discussed it at a scheduled meeting in the kitchenette. Reading the book riled all of us up.

Lóa was adamant that the book was exploitative, a male author monetising love between women: these authors were in a crisis, she said, they had filled libraries with male problems that no longer surprised anyone and had now run out of things to write about, except perhaps the experiences of men who desire to become women – therein lay a fresh male challenge whose depths had yet to be plumbed.

Lóa's fiancé heartily agreed.

Úrsúla gave authors the right to write about anything, regardless of culture and origin. An author shouldn't matter so much – the book itself, the artwork itself, was the core, or the centre. Were she in charge, she would eradicate author names from all artworks.

'What do you mean by exploitation?' Nói said.

'To exploit for one's own benefit the wellspring of those who have fewer or no opportunities to discover their own spring, and to reap its rewards,' Magnea said.

'Pain is a source of power – pain is one's diamond. I won't

have someone else profiting from mine,' Lóa said and looked crossly at her fiancé, who blinked. 'Men covet the pain reserves of women, which have gone up in value. As soon as the value of any female reserve increases, they begin to covet it, even if previously it was considered worthless. Or rather, previously there were no reserves, only hunger and dumping grounds.'

Kristinn Logi had no faith in the imagination, as we knew, and the book did nothing to change his position, even if the author had an easy time putting himself into the shoes of women. But as a man, how could Kristinn know that? asked Lóa. He couldn't, of course, replied Kristinn, and added that queer love was currently in fashion in the entertainment industry.

Magnea thought the sex scenes seemed tainted by the private fantasies of the male author, but that overall it was pretty well done.

Úrsúla felt there were too many sex scenes: 'They do nothing for me.'

Magnea agreed and added that the author had written those scenes just for himself and his friends, to prove to them how emotionally sensitive he was and good at understanding women.

'What are private fantasies?' I asked.

Axel said that all fantasies are private, communal fantasies do not exist. Lóa said that fantasies are universal and far from mysterious.

'Books are meant to preserve communal human perception,' Kristinn Logi explained.

'I call into question the adjective *human* and the noun *hu-*

manity,' Magnea said. 'The words sound good but the truth is that humanity never reveals itself without cruelty.'

Nói patted Magnea's shoulder. 'Now, now.'

'That being said, I trust the word *humane* to bring good into the world,' she said, and shrank away from the patting.

'Fantasies are always worth cataloguing,' said Úrsúla. She worshipped the human and the humane – everything that humans produced in the field of art, female, male, neuter or androgynous, and all other fruits of the forest – the human was beauty itself, like all life-forms on the planet. But she was a special admirer of mankind and of creation in its entirety.

Axel said that democracy had rejected the book, since it didn't sell. Authors like Úlfur Högnason would have fared better under a monarchy, Magnea said, and reminded everyone that the book's production had been subsidised by the state.

'State grants heal the wounds left by capitalism,' Úrsúla said, kings were better patrons of the arts than plutocrats.

Lóa didn't see the difference: plutocrats – merchants – kings – hangmen of democracy – they all used art as propaganda, and the arts, in their frailty and need for acceptance and acknowledgment, served as devoted lapdogs to the powers that be.

No one said 'come, now,' or 'now, now,' and patted Lóa on the shoulder, but Axel embraced her. Nói expressed his admiration for the phrase *hangmen of democracy*. I didn't understand it. We agreed that the book's cultural critique was sharp, and discussed whether the author might possibly have been familiar with the inner workings of the unit.

Kristinn Logi knew through the heads of the Ministry of Education that the publisher had been advised by anonymous individuals within the system – within what system, we didn't know exactly – to curb interest in the book, which was badly written and inconsistent. We agreed that the descriptions of the hero's narcotic delirium were inventive, the dialogue stiff.

In the Winter Garden

The nights got shorter and the mornings repeated themselves save that it got brighter earlier: I awoke – 6.20, checked my wristwatch for confirmation, got out of bed, looked for my glasses, swept aside the curtains, tore the seal between day and night: the mountain appeared before me like a truck stuck in its tracks. I compared the light with the morning glimmer of the week past and the one before that and the one before that and took a cat bath, or a shower; drank the coffee that I had accustomed myself to drinking in the mornings, drank it by a shining blue steel sink that exterminated all possibility of mould in the kitchen; watched from my kitchen window as the hard rain changed into disoriented snowflakes, which quickly found their bearings and drove down, then lost their bearings and turned into drizzle, a mist that grew thinner and thinner while I repeated myself and repeated myself, having long since given up searching for my archetype or trying to cast a new mould.

I arrived punctually to work each day, greeted the security guard couple in the ministry foyer, worked in my corner on my report on stand-up comedy on the city's stages during winter 20XX–20XX, took coffee and lunch breaks in the kitchenette, chatted, listened to other people's conversations, chatted more and listened to more wonderful chatter and kept myself and kept myself and kept myself within the prescribed limits. In the afternoon I walked along the ocean, never went beyond the city limits to the green lake, came home early and cooked dinner.

Dinner.

Dinner.

The contents of the egg that the swanfolk had sent us, or me, at the Special Unit, grew and flourished inside a bullet-proof warming box in the laboratory of the state's pathology department, under security cameras, covered in monitors. The first ultrasound revealed a creature with a bird's lower half and webbed feet, and a human torso, arms and head. Its heartbeat resembled that of a human. Further ultrasounds were unable to confirm the sex of the broodling. Employees on round-the-clock shifts monitored its healthy development. Cardiologists regularly examined its charts and listened to its heartbeat.

Late

on a Wednesday,

20 April

if I remember correctly, on the birthday of a German mass murderer, as someone had undoubtedly pointed out in the kitchenette, less than two weeks after the egg arrived, Selma and I arranged to meet in the Winter Garden, which was within walking distance of my house, about a thirty-minute journey at normal walking speed. The garden was meant for owners to let their dogs run around unbridled and was known informally as the Dog Park. For the past thirteen days the sun had been held backstage by endless tangles of clouds, but it was shining just then and higher aloft than before, and wouldn't be setting until roughly an hour after dinner.

Rex, who followed me from home, disappeared through the park gate. I positioned myself next to a white litter bin on coarse gravel and waited for my boss, whom I wasn't comfortable calling my friend, and got lost in looking at the unbelievably blue sky. This colour couldn't possibly appear anywhere but in a dream. East of the hill, on the other side of the highway, the swanfolk would be sitting in a hidden glade under the same blue sky. From where they sat a half rainbow stretched upward like a machete. Was spring finally here?

Nah – Selma didn't think so, and she slammed the front door of the dark-blue car she had arrived in, stirring up dust; I coughed – it wouldn't be here just yet, the sun was still struggling to break through the pot lid covering the North Pole, which was nearly impenetrable; meteorologists didn't see another sunny day on the cards in the coming weeks.

'These clouds refuse to unravel. Meteorologists have never seen such unyielding clouds, which have taken it upon themselves to protect the Arctic's armada, the sea ice, from the sun's rays – which in and of itself isn't bad, but it delays the growth of all vegetation considerably,' she added, and put on the red leather gloves that Venus gave Rósa to mark a special occasion and which Selma therefore had on a kind of loan. For a quick minute we unbuttoned our coats and performed a weapons check on each other. Her hips had widened. We buttoned our coats back up. The shadows tugged us through the arched gate created by the intermingling branches of two birch trees a few metres over our heads. Selma stuck her hand through my arm and into my coat pocket. It was too intimate to ask why she was happy, so I asked instead whether she had made any plans for the summer vacation – no, what about me? no – she asked when I was going to stop wearing these rubber boots – soon.

The path twisted along a sheer and craggy shoreline. Across a grass-green open field were scattered a handful of slim trees. The colour of the sea – a deep-dim blue – and the ice-white sea foam pointed like the forecast map to the obstinacy of winter. The wind grabbed at Selma's hair.

'I feel amazing,' she admitted, 'I haven't felt like this since I was ten years old – by twelve, it was all over – until suddenly now I feel wonderful. Life is marvellous, Frankó.' She tucked her hair behind her ear but the wind wouldn't give up and it was blown loose again and again and again. The wind also tried as it could to claim our coats while Selma elucidated: 'The mind instinctively dispels ugly thoughts. At night I lie on my pillow and ask for worries to come, but they don't answer my call – there is no room for worries in my body. If Venus calls – which he does once Dóra has gone to bed; he goes onto the balcony, pretends to smoke – and wants to discuss the relationship, I don't get annoyed, I just start laughing. If he wants to come over I say: Oh, just come. If I don't want him to come over I say: Don't come now – without explanation. If he is upset I just laugh. Isn't it bizarre, Frankó?'

Yes, but at the same time I thought it inappropriate to remind her of the pregnancy.

'But how is the representative of the swanfolk doing?'

Her joy, which functioned like a new element in the world, irritated me – a typical reaction of bystanders to new joy – but hopefully I did not let on.

'Fine.'

'Good,' she said and leaned up against me. 'Remember the other day when Lóa was asking us in the kitchenette whether we had ever gotten a new bed with all new bedding at the same time?'

Yes, I vaguely remembered Lóa's informal survey. Because of their wedding this summer they wanted to know whether people get themselves a new bed – with all new everything – when they get married or at some other point in their lives. Neither Selma nor I had ever got a new bed with all new everything, we had both scraped all the accessories together over a long period of time, and the same was true of our colleagues. Venus disappeared before it was his turn to be polled and I interpreted that as an act of politeness, to protect Rósa's feelings.

'Venus explained to me later at a secret meeting,' she added, 'what it's like being a new couple in a new apartment, with new flooring, freshly painted walls, new kitchen fittings and new pots and pans – it's like walking around in a steel paradise. Then the couple takes a bath in a bathtub that no one has ever bathed in before, dries themselves with new towels made from the very best cotton, all the pipes brand-new so the water is clear and the electricity reliable, the beds outfitted with new duvets filled with new, hand-picked down. In an environment that is brand-new like that the body's need to be a body grows, he said, and is endowed with a new power that wants to express its primal instinct, tear the towels apart, assert itself over the paint on the walls, make love for days until the paint flakes off. Do you know what he means?'

'No.'

'When you wake up after the first night you feel like a freshly polished robot. Don't you think that's a beautiful description?'

'Yes.'

'Then I said to Venus,' Rósa laughed, 'my love, how I long to throw up in a brand-new toilet.' She tugged at my coat pocket. 'But I wasn't joking, Frankó. Now Venus dreams of moving for the second time in his life, with me and the new baby into a new house with all new everything in it; he only wants to live in rooms where the walls are widescreen. In order to grow up, a child needs to sleep at least a few nights in an old house without a fridge, without electricity, I told him, and then he said he didn't know whether he trusted me with his son. He has five daughters,' she laughed. All of us at the Special Unit knew that Venus had five daughters, sometimes they came to visit him at work. 'He gave me three weeks to think it over.'

'Yes,' I replied and looked out onto the old-fangled or new-fangled ocean. How I wanted to get to the bottom of the blue of the sky.

'I seem to be making a half-decent primipara – I'm not suffering from nausea or having any discomfort.'

'Yes,' I replied.

'And before, I never kissed Venus at work, but now I do but never on the mouth, not while I'm pregnant. Are pregnant women grossed out by kisses, Frankó?'

I pretended to have read that a woman became a sacred temple while she was with child. We sat down on a bench. She drew a banana from her coat pocket. I waited excitedly for her to point out the arch of anxiety that obviously lay on the horizon and which the sun tried to conceal.

'Maybe I'll get an abortion – anyway, the deadline hasn't passed. I have never wanted to give birth to a child,' she said.

'Me neither,' I said.

'It's so nice to sit with you on a bench, Frankó.'

'Thanks, likewise, Rósa.'

'Frankó, will the happiness disappear if I get an abortion?'

'I just don't know, Rósa.'

'I doubt it will last forever. Should we investigate that at the unit?'

'Whether joy during pregnancy is invincible?'

'I'm going to miss it.'

'I can't be near people who eat bananas in public,' I said and she laughed, threw the banana in the bin and wiped her mouth with a gentleman's handkerchief.

We walked back without speaking or touching. Our paths diverged at the gate. She said she had to go to an important soirée at the Tower, some kind of rite of spring. The car stirred up dust. I coughed.

In the Tower

An hour later – I didn't go home in the meantime, but wandered around the neighbourhood, desperate for air, and looked for Rex – I was sitting in a limousine with my superiors: Selma Mjöll in a lacy, light-blue dress, and Helgi Björn in a tuxedo. From a chamois leather bag she offered me a pair of sandals. When I was little I would dress my paper dolls, themed from antiquity, in sandals. This silver pair was more suitable for a space age. I took off my rubber boots.

'Should I wear my socks?' I asked Selma, who was barefoot in golden, open-toed shoes. It was up to me. Rósa opened her palm when Venus moved his closer. Their palms, united, formed a shell. Light quivered on her earrings and his cufflinks. He wanted to kiss her. The window between us and the driver went one-way, only we could see through it.

The lampposts in my city were so beautiful. Soon the season would offer them a few weeks' holiday as daylight seized control from the night. Beauty is always impractical, utility never glistens – so said a French schoolmistress in a lecture back when the world could still afford to squander its reserves.

In our times, beauty is considered healthy, useful, civic and organised, Magnea had once explained in the kitchenette. We sail on leafsails, Mum had said. I admired the lampposts in my beautiful city while we drove over a roundabout, past giant buildings on gaping side streets arranged in squares that had yet to be boarded up with windowpanes. Gulls floated on the air. I didn't bother to ask whether there was any news of the golden plover on the country's eastern shores.

'Frankó, we're done kissing, you can look now,' announced Rósa.

'Good,' I didn't reply.

'Today I read an article, which I will send you both,' said Helgi Björn. 'It's about a technique to read from people's lips whether they are lying or telling the truth. The author prides himself on being able to discern between truth and falsehood in ninety-nine per cent of cases without assistance from a computer. There are simple instructions.'

He moved her fringe more gently than the wind.

'The three of us are good together,' Venus added, and Rósa smiled.

I weighed the lie and truth encompassed by her smile. Her joy couldn't have dissipated in just the past hour, not according to her previous descriptions and declarations.

'You two are my favourite travel companions. How I'll always remember the trip to Paris. Wasn't that when you were attacked?' he said, and meant me.

'It was then,' replied Selma.

The vehicle came quietly to a halt like a footless animal. The driver opened the back door and held it open. Selma climbed out first, Helgi followed me, nodded to the driver, the door shut v e r y slowly and my closeness to the car turned all too quickly into a fictive distance that, like the closeness itself, could never materialise, no promises.

The Tower seemed to widen the higher up it went.

On the plaza outside I discovered a new perspective and a different orientation of time and space. It felt as if time and space had not yet decided what they were, and in the meantime deceived us – inside this interval, just before the decision was made – and mocked us with a feeling of vertigo that I admired and succumbed to. We walked through a rose-gold revolving door and then a gate that fired rays through our bags, clothes and bodies; past the security guards who watched over the inner cameras, dressed in grey uniforms piped with gold, and into a hall larger than any I had ever been inside, fortified with polished timber. The ceiling and floor were adorned with shells beneath a mounted membrane of frost. Guards assisted us out of our coats and in exchange for mine handed me a red token with a number on it.

People in formal wear received us with open arms. Helgi Björn and Selma Mjöll introduced me to some, said that I was in charge of the unit's anthropological investigations as well as security matters on the third floor of the ministry. The air smelled of flowers and glistened of eyes, ears and fingertips, hair, teeth, lips.

The police chief told the secretary that I was a key employee of the Special Unit and that my parents, who disappeared at a symposium abroad, had conducted important research on languages, including the impact of language on the sexual maturity of mammals, if he remembered correctly – yes. 'I'm sorry for your loss,' he said, and bowed.

'Me too,' I said, 'but maybe it was for their best.'

The police chief, civilly dressed in a dark suit, on which hung a medallion, didn't hear my addendum. The minister of the interior, wearing a blue dress, held a long white stole and smiled. Young people, some in ornate dresses and others in breeches and yellow vests, with caps and bells on their heads, greeted the minister and the chief. Giggling, they said they were dressed for the apocalypse and selling tickets to an end-of-the-world lottery.

The secretary and the chief laughed along and bought a ticket each. The youths disappeared into the crowd, the minister and the chief disappeared into a group of tuxedos and I, left standing alone, said the following:

'They were investigating which language brought its users happiness. They told my brother Unnar that in Europe the French language came closest to offering a feeling of freedom – or the least far from it, I can't remember which – as well as passable tools to think with. They said our mother tongue possessed the tenderest words in the Indo-European languages: *rest* – how tender the word sounds. *Endure. Friend* – so much love lies within that word, they said. *Prithee eat me, my friend.* They said that harsh or draconian societies – I can't remember which adjective they used, or my brother did in his retelling – had the most comprehensive collections of soft and tender sounds:

'Bode, be, be with me, bewithmetonightmylove, don'tbesad, sadness – equally soft as an adjective and a noun. *Hope. Blossom. Ghost. Aghast. Whine. Wail* – plenty of *wailing* in *wail. Wont. Colt. Bolt. Relentless. Stop. Shop. Chop. Chops. Flesh. Skin. Sod. Dusk. Bane. Sill. Shadow.* But which adjective is more beautiful, *pretty* or *handsome*? Mum would ask Dad.

Pretty, Mum would say.

Handsome, Dad would say.

Then she would change her mind. *Handsome* has a more real – no, a more believable beauty than *pretty*.

Resound. Misted. Winded. Ode. Use. Ply. Beget. Oblation. Blood. Sin. Swim. Moment. Hand. Grove. Sleepy. Wind. Blind. Magic –

Mum would ask: Can you hear, my children, how the words taste sweet as dates? And are softer than any sleeping pill?

To live. Even the verb *to die* sounds like a French skipping rope.

They were on their way out of Europe when they disappeared . . .'

Waiters filled glasses from green bottles and served multi-coloured cakes on silver platters. Inside the lights and refractions illuminating the hall danced tiny dots of light, some like horizontal snowflakes at a calm gallop, others moving at a sedative pace. My female boss stood across from me and talked to people dressed in cassocks and red glimmerdresses. Barefooted, long-haired teenagers entered the hall holding hands, wearing pale lace dresses, with flower wreaths on their heads. They disappeared into the crowd.

'Were you talking to yourself, Elísabet?' a female voice asked.

'Huh?'

'Were you talking to yourself?'

Lóa and Axel positioned themselves in front of me. They were holding hands.

'Yes, you *were* talking to yourself,' Lóa insisted.

No. Hi. Did they come to the Tower often? Sometimes, but definitely not too often. I had never been before and didn't know my purpose, did they know theirs?

'We attend receptions to practise being a married couple,' Axel said. 'You know about our wedding this summer, if summer ever comes. A couple needs to practise being a couple, even socially.'

I had never before seen them holding hands.

'It's because in the Tower we practise,' Lóa added. According to personality tests her weaknesses lay in the social realm. Her psychiatrist recommended practice: attending events and strengthening their team unity and her social skills.

Axel whispered in my ear: 'In any case, you know better than anyone that our primary role here is to pay attention, listen to conversations, get respondents to forget themselves and speak carelessly.'

Was my role one of surveillance? On the ride over my superiors didn't mention anything about what I was doing here. Were they exhibiting me?

Some of the young people in ornate dresses and breeches and jester's caps ran over to us:

'May we dress you up, jumper girl?' they said. *Jumper girl*. They spun me around 180 degrees, placed a garland of flowers around my neck, and draped over my shoulders a short silver cape.

'Tonight we dress for the end of the world, celebrate life, face death in our finery –'

They said.

I bought a ticket for the apocalottery with the loose change in my pocket. The young people disappeared into the crowd. Suddenly I thought I saw my sister Æsa among them and pushed my way through the swarm of people, searched for her face and found instead the back of a group of tall, broad and bowlegged men wearing suits variously coloured red,

orange,

yellow,

green,

blue,

purple, their hair and beards neatly trimmed, diamonds in their ears – their pain in their ears – white trainers. They kneeled and played cat's cradle with barefooted children wearing lace dresses coloured purple,

blue,

green,

yellow,

orange,

red. I could see that they wore leotards under their dresses, their hair tied up in ponytails or buns.

A group of older women stormed in wearing floor-length dresses – some black, others gold – as well as golden sandals, toes painted in rainbows. They were accompanied by young men in sailor suits carrying thick furs, each and every one with a beauty mark just left of the mouth, and silver eyelashes.

An ornate band walked into the hall, barely able to lift their instruments. The director of the National Book Inventory, Natan Laufeyjarson himself, drew from his top hat a white handkerchief, waved to me, and introduced me to his wife, Lára, a thin, small-boned lady in a floral dress. She held his arm. He whispered to me that I would have to read her lips since her vocal cords had snapped. When I introduced myself she nodded, and if I read her lips correctly said:

'Unnardóttir – you know, I knew your mother. She taught me to read and write.'

Lára squeezed my upper arm.

'That's nice to hear,' I replied.

'And you know, Elísabet, I didn't need to learn anything more.'

Natan drew Lára away. She waved to me. In the same breath, Nói Ingason ran over, his eyes black, his tongue purple.

'Elísabet, you're here, hi.'

He embraced me and whispered in my ear: 'Earlier I heard that in the upper echelons of the ministry they call me Yo-yo.' Then rushed off wearing his navy-blue jacket, with a silver cape like mine on his shoulders, his lined with red sequined cloth.

The barefoot teenagers in the pale floral dresses and flower crowns stepped onto the stage and launched into a circle dance accompanied by classic American love songs from days of yore played on trumpet by teenagers in green elfin costume.

'I want to die in the arms of my commander,' shouted a

dressed-up old codger, holding the hand of another dressed-up old codger who laughed and shouted: 'Me too, my good man,' and tuned his hearing aid, or turned it off.

'With the new municipal plans comes increased regulation of communication and transportation – the two go hand in hand in every city in the world – as well as, of course, improved surveillance,' said someone wearing a blue suit.

'This modern age has been capricious and chaotic, but with increased transparency we secure a prosperous future,' said someone in a red dress.

'According to our analytics, there is no need to fear unrest,' said someone in a white suit.

'This has been a singular age. In truth it's surprising how satisfied the people are. A toast to a singular age.' The one in the blue suit raised his glass and the one in the white suit added:

'It takes three decades for resentment to take root, proliferate, and supplant hopes and dreams, but by always being three steps ahead . . .'

The interlocutors were interrupted by a pair of lieutenants or colonels who suddenly appeared beside them. I didn't see Æsa anywhere. A troop of seniors who did research and ran errands for the unit were engaged in spirited conversation, throwing their arms around, eyebrows thick as wirework, their silver heads glimmeringly beautiful. On the dance floor Axel and Lóa practised their ballroom dancing. If I came across my lady boss I would invite her to dance. Then Dr Bónus bent down over me on heaven-high heels and asked how things were going with my hallucinations. Her dress was braided with strings of pearls, her hair with purple and red feathers.

'They weren't hallucinations,' I replied, 'but I am sworn to secrecy and can't say any more.' And I laughed in the same way I saw the other guests laughing and didn't feel I was being insincere. Had I matured? Perhaps I would accept the promotion after all and shoulder responsibility like a fully formed citizen?

Dr Bónus nearly twisted my arm and looked sternly into my eyes, her teeth straight and true: 'Do me a favour and be careful, Elísabet Eva, multiple-resistant bacteria are multiplying in the atmosphere at a rate no one expected.'

She let me go, looked across the dance floor to where a man in a light-grey suit and cowboy boots waited for her, then headed over. As she embraced him I was met briefly with a bloodshot glare. The couple glided, in step, onto the dance floor. Among the dancers I thought I saw my brother, Unnar, and his fiancée, Þorsteina Margrét, but deemed it a figment of my imagination, a hallucination, wishful thinking. Nói ran over carrying a puppy, grabbed on to me to keep himself from falling over:

'They called me Yo-yo because they thought my name was Jói. Just think, Elísabet, all the geniuses who came up with words like *yo-yo*, *submissive*, *petunia*, *snapdragon*, and all the idioms – *As good be an addled egg as an idle bird!*'

He vanished before I could ask where he'd got the puppy.

The dancers, singers, and trumpeters disappeared into the wings. Onto the stage stepped five comics, each of whom had a paragraph devoted to them in the draft of my report on the local scene, wearing dark clothes and large white wigs. Four of them danced a minuet. The fifth pointed and waved a gun.

———

THE FIRST: 'Upon hearing of the death of a friend, I feel the truth laid bare: the world offers no one a safe place to stay. Disposed of the house. Take a seat on the wretched square. Will die for nothing more than some dirty lingerie.'

THE SECOND: 'It's barely worth taking my clothes from their case. For the sake of repetition, I repeat myself. Dreams soothe the heart, but they don't put food on your plate. I get up for chocolate tart and attack the world with beauty as a way of raising hell. No, of saying farewell.'

THIRD: 'My love knew no bigger fool than I. Truly she was the apple of my thoughts and my eye. I lived to make her suffer beautifully and eat chocolate tart. She thought for us. I played my part.'

FOURTH: 'Kiss, kissing, kissed, yes, my love, a kiss and a kiss and a kiss. Goodbye, bye, bathe you, yes, bathe you, bye, little flower of my bliss.'

FIFTH: (*having drawn a gun, aimed and fired at the wigs of the other comics, which caught fire*) 'Oh, do I hear correctly? What do stupid clowns say? Does a scientific journal measure, or a childish imbecile! Hey ho, dear sweet well-behaved tarts. Are those tears of blood or sweat? Bang bang! Where the hell's your funny bone, funnyman? Bang bang! I don't know many words, but what I have I use better than a naked comic who can't even knit.'

FIRST: 'My love, may I torment you one last time? Oh, what's this? Flowers, for me?'

SECOND: 'Please, be my guest, the hour of our departure's

drawing near. Without chocolate tarts we are mere ephemera. You sweet sweeter sweetest nobody.'

THIRD: 'Let's say goodbye, because it's crueller to meet and crueller to wake than it is to sleep, which can mean only one thing: you can live without death's rattle shake.'

FOURTH: 'The memory wipes out moments of luck and celebrates sorrow. The birth is forgotten, death perseveres. How will we survive beyond tomorrow without dangling from repetition like a chandelier?'

FIFTH: (*lighting his own wig on fire*) 'Everything is so horribly hopeless and rotten – bang! Rotten country, rotten irony!'

Special forces stormed the stage and extinguished the flaming wigs. Paramedics followed with stretchers. Selma Mjöll came over and reminded me that I had recommended these so-called comics. The teenagers in the lace dresses flocked onto the stage with bouquets and dumped them onto the comics, who were being helped onto the stretchers. 'Deeply disturbed comics,' Selma added.

The entertainers that I had lauded in the draft of my report were carried off the stage. The interior minister was heading my way. Selma gave me a signal to leave. The choir of teenagers spread out over the stage along with the trumpet players. Makeup was running down the face of a woman standing nearby. The group that together formed a rainbow of suits had got wet and their fingers had become entangled in the cat's cradle strings. Two girls screamed at each other. The old codgers stood close to one another, whispering with their hands in their pockets. A young man in a light-grey suit poured red wine from a cowboy boot over his head. One bare foot. Another young man in a light-grey suit poured red wine from a cowboy boot over his chest and crotch. One bare foot. I walked to the cloak-room, handed the lady in the black lace dress my red token and asked whether she had worked in the Tower for long, but didn't receive a response other than my coat in my face.

It was prohibited to exit the way we had come in. I pulled a few handles on doors that appeared to be fashioned out of shells, all locked. Then I followed a waiter who disappeared underneath the stage. From there I walked along underground passageways, past an enormous kitchen made of steel and a stockroom with long shelves full of cakes and cold steel boxes. In a meat locker hung game carcasses numbering in the thou-sands. In the workshop a couple of janitors painted signs. Two boys in blue delivery uniforms, with yellow baseball caps, sat playing cards in the laundry room and pointed me to the doors that let me out.

The sun greeted me in the stairs leading up from the base-ment.

In a glamorous alleyway there was nothing to see except a couple of tidy blue rubbish bins, which I climbed onto, end-ing up on the other side of the wall by the highway, on a slim pavement suitable for the ambulations of an animal such as a rat. A row of ambulances – I counted five – disappeared down the sloping hill. I ran across the highway without getting tan-gled in a chorus of car horns; the light traffic suggested it was dinnertime in my country.

Wedding

'What lovely silver sandals you're wearing,' Fjóla whispered and stuck her head up out of the reeds beneath the green bench, after I had sat for a moment and eaten some of the little cakes I had stuffed into my pockets at the Tower. I offered some to Fjóla. When the sun disappeared below the horizon it got colder, but I was feeling cocky and willing to put up with pottering around in sandals.

'I just came from a party, and will you look at this,' I said and took off my coat, showed Fjóla the silver cape and the garland of flowers, draped the former over her shoulders and the latter around her neck.

'Wow, how lovely I look. You know, many thought you wouldn't come to the wedding, and many thought you would,' she said and pondered the small red cake that she had selected from the pile, asked whether they were called macaroons in my language. Yes. She had never tasted macaroons before.

'Wedding?' I asked, like an idiot.

Yes, the swanfolk had placed bets on whether I would show up to the wedding of Mikki and Móa, but she would never reveal the ratios, only that she was on the winning team.

'It's lonely belonging to neither the winning nor losing team. Let's give those who didn't take part in the bet the rest of the cakes,' she said, and swept the macaroons into a bag. 'The human goes from one party to the next.'

Fjóla looked left and right, ran across the empty path and disappeared between the trees. I followed. We walked the same way we had eleven days prior, over the hill, the next one, and down and up a third. Beyond it we came to a pond that I had never seen before or since, on walks or maps. On the pond I could see the bride and groom, Mikael and Móa, and bridesmaids around them – among them Álfrún Perla, Blíng and Kósetta, adorned with pine branches. They sang. Ástríður Petra and the leader waved to me and Fjóla at the same time as they jumped from the bank into the water. Fjóla filled a platter with macaroons and floated it on the pond. She dove in as I sat down on the ground and fished the binoculars from my bag.

A shower of dry snow fell from the sky.

Torches and pyres made of sticks, twigs and tree branches floated on a raft on the pond, and on another raft covered in a tablecloth I saw through my binoculars a stack of pink buns, worm salad in shells, and jars filled with worm wine.

The bridegroom's body was strapped to a wooden stake, fastened with branches and rope decorated with bows. That's how the corpse was kept upright. He wore a top hat. A veil made of a black net covered Móa's face. Her bridal gown was of the same material and decorated with bric-a-brac, shells, bows and stones.

'We had to let Móa have her wedding,' said Lena, who all of a sudden stood beside me, along with María.

'Yes, we had to let Móa have her wedding,' María repeated.

They wore coats made of nets, ornamented with glittering necklaces and chains made of twigs, shells and straw. They joined in the singing and trumpeting that drifted from the pond. It looked to me like Fjóla was the one blowing the trumpet. Kornlilja played a guitar, someone else a drum, another threw me a bun, which I caught without dropping the binoculars. Lena and María jumped into the water and were met by Mandý and Soffía, who carried lit torches and proceeded to light the pyres that floated on the water. They looked like burning flowers.

The bride took the mittened hands of her groom, brought them to her lips and kissed them. Ástríður Petra draped a necklace around the bride's neck. The top hat fell into the water. Soffía lit it on fire. The groom's fastenings gave out. Slowly the corpse slumped into the lake. The leader waved a torch and kindled the branches and fastenings around his body. The bridegroom's finery smoldered like the torches in the hands of the swanmaidens, and the ones floating on the water and the funeral pyre. Everything blazed. Then I looked up at the live broadcast of the darkness moving across the sky as cold stiffened the earth and the ground fractured with a little crack. The hills and the trees waited suspensefully for night, for it to lay itself carefully and decidedly over them. The singing and music faded slowly. Then nothing was left but the sounds of swimming and gurgling. In a split second the fire turned to smoke, the pond grew pitch-dark, the sky and the earth became one – the sky begot the earth and the earth begot the sky. The odd fragment of birdsong carried from a distant nest and from trees farther afield. It was almost as if the water had swallowed everything and the earth had swallowed the water. The balance between heaven and earth was absolute. I could see nothing of the water when I illuminated my surroundings with a flashlight. In the air there hung a faint smell of burning. I waited for a long while until I tired of hearing nothing, then bit into the bun: oh, it was a regular pink-glazed bun you could get at any bakery in the city. Out loud I called the names of Álfrún Perla, Ástríður Petra, Blíng, Fjóla, Kornlilja, Kósetta, Lena, Mandý, María, Mikael, Móa, Soffía, the nameless leader (I called out: Leader!), and, just in case, the names of Órekur and Earl Prince Karl. Nothing and no one answered, except for a raven that chirped as it flew and got farther away. Everything was quiet, calm, serene, over.

As I made my way back the moon poked out between clouds and lit up the hills. I looked over my shoulder. No pond. My phone rang, and how the ring resembled a chirp. I grabbed hold of a branch before answering it. Selma asked whether I was all right. I lowered my voice and tried to conceal my shortness of breath: everything was just dandy, I said, and asked her the same. All fine. I could hear in her voice that she had company. I asked about my rain boots, she promised to bring them to work tomorrow, I would bring the sandals; no, she said, they were a gift – and it wasn't the first time Selma had gifted me shoes. Good thing I hadn't taken my socks off in the limousine.

She asked whether she ought to pick me up tomorrow morning, surely I couldn't get to work in sandals – no no, I would find myself a pair of shoes down in the storeroom.

'Are you outside?'

'On the balcony.'

'But your apartment doesn't have a balcony,' Selma complained.

I pulled on a branch.

'The steps outside are called a balcony, apparently.'

We wished each other good night.

I listened for sounds and looked back. No pond. The charged hum or taut rustling of sleep over the land touched a mysterious force and impulses in my body that I sated by whistling a little ditty and getting a move on. Tangled in crooked branches, heather and knotted roots, I somehow walked over the hills without falling too often and arrived back at the path, which sparkled with tiny frostwork, then crossed an empty highway.

TWISTS & TURNS

20 April–?

Atonement, Reproach, Shame, Disgrace, Dishonour –
ALL THE BEAUTIFUL WORDS

By the living room window I sat down on a chair that had belonged to my parents – and that my brother Unnar had encouraged me to keep, since objects preserve memories – and soaked my feet in hot water. A frost had ridden on the heels of twilight. On a hardened snowbank in the back garden a pair of tracks made by a baby carriage glowed in the moonlight. A toy bucket and spade towered crookedly on the snowbank's highest peak. Sometimes at night my upstairs neighbour would sit in their dressing gown on the whalebone in the garden and read on their phone while I sat in the memory chair and read old messages on mine. Thoughts intruded and changed nothing. Time had not opened my eyes to aspects of my actions beyond those I could justify, and my thinking didn't see straight.

Dear thought, I asked my thought, surprise me and take the reins, because if she who holds the whip is left in charge, you, dear thoughts, will never wake me to awareness. Please open my eyes and show me another way – or else lead me astray.

Is it a crime to correct the résumé of a ballerina who danced at a strip club not far from Parliament, if one discovers that she never completed formal dance training like she had claimed under interrogation – thereby giving the authorities a viable and convenient reason to deport her?

How does one wash one's hands?

Does one quiet one's conscience by appealing to one's vanity, with an exceptionally well-cut beard, with cufflinks, clothing style, footwear, a ponytail?

Is it possible to be a proud citizen of a nation of people who turn their backs in unison on those who fall behind, and cast the vulnerable out to sea?

I dried my feet and laid my head, disappointed – or not disappointed, so thin was the difference, and yet I had more than enough excuses up my sleeve to improve my mood – onto my pillow.

If I were a viewer of the film of my life, what would I choose to see? Not a darkened screen where you could just make out the silhouette of a window curtain and, before it, a dim mass that is the bed. No, I would prefer to see a scene on roller skates. Then I fell asleep.

From the Egg

The draft of my report about the local stand-up scene in winter 20XX–20XX, which I had worked on many of the previous weeks, was rendered obsolete by the performance at the Tower. The following day I requested another extension, yet another deadline, from my boss. It was readily granted when I appeared at Selma Mjöll's office early that morning. The rubber boots of my mother, grandma, or sister Æsa stood on the table. Selma's voice was hoarse, her lipstick pink.

The importance of the report had increased as a consequence of the performance, she said and pecked at her keyboard. The quintet had been checked into accident and emergency following the stand-up routine that was not a stand-up routine, rather a performance piece and a dance – 'Minuet,' she said, and shook her head. Technically they had prepared the piece well, the safety equipment for the fires in the wigs was exemplary; the group had an engineer in their midst but no psychologist or psychiatrist. They had neglected to account for the mental repercussions of such a magnificent and difficult performance – a performance that went further in its irrational foolery than scrupulous and perfectionist performers could withstand.

'Did you understand any of what they were saying?' she said.

'Not really.'

'Natan on the fifth floor is extremely fond, he told me so on the phone last night. He says it is art and so it must be art.'

'Yes,' I said and nodded, 'then it must be art.'

'They probably couldn't handle the pressure. Comics like them belong on smaller stages in front of smaller crowds, in charming basement theatres with red curtains and a grimy bar, you know,' she said and looked at a watch on her wrist. 'As we speak they are being driven out of the city to convalesce at a sanitarium out east. All's well that ends well. The report will be of use when it's finished, not least to the comics themselves,' Selma promised.

We discussed the possibility of my being allowed to interview them at the sanitarium. Then I pointed to the scales, which tilted less in favour of capital than the other week. We must be doing something right. She nodded, waved a pencil:

'Even though people don't know the unit exists, they trust us,' she said, and brought the meeting to a close.

I stood in the glass doors with my boots in my arms, contemplated Selma as she tapped her keyboard, dressed in a new, brine-blue dress patterned with white waves, when suddenly a departmental alarm went off. Everyone on the floor was immediately filed into a white van and driven down to the state's pathology department. Those were some of our best moments together, being driven in the four-row minibus between institutions and departments on urgent business. The same people always sat by the window, in the middle, in the front, but I won't divulge the exact seating arrangement.

In the span of an hour the shell of the egg cracked open, the nestling tore off its membrane revealing a creature with the same build as those I knew by the water. A round of applause bid the marvel hatchling welcome to the world, but the chick could almost certainly not hear the clapping through the thick glass cupola around its nest. It shook its head as if emerging from water, its eyes broke their way through the slime that glued its lids shut. Assistants in hazmat suits stepped into the thermal locker, washed the hatchling, took its vital signs, and ran preliminary tests.

'Selene,' Axel proposed naming the nestling, 'or Endymion,' he added, because its sex had not yet been confirmed by the specialists.

'Hope,' Selma Mjöll suggested.

'Swanlass,' Magnea said.

'Swanchild,' said Helgi Björn and looked lovingly at Selma Mjöll – or, more accurately, said Venus and looked lovingly at Rósa – sent a secret message with the glimmer in his eye. Úrsúla wrote down the names that sounded around the room in a communal thoughtstorm:

Swanmaiden, Maidenbloom, Hopeling, Princeling, Starling, Stella, Estelle, Astra, Aster, Aenon, Seren, Starblossom, Arno, Ren, Waterblossom, Moonstone, Elpis, Honour, Annora, Alvina, Elfswan, Elwyn, Swanwyn, Marlowe, Tallulah, Ondine, Cressida, Chryses, Cobling, Penling.

Nói: 'Watermaiden or Watersquire.'

Lóa: 'Wingmaiden.'

Kristinn Logi: 'Swanald.'

I would have named the hatchling Dimmalimm, Prince, or Dimmalimo, but I had had enough, pretended to need the restroom, didn't understand why I had had enough now that the proof of my story had appeared for all to see, bona fide and born from an egg, and I fled the premises.

What had upset me? The happiness and excitement of my colleagues? The namestorm? The hatchling itself? The communal hallucination?

My alien feelings and unwillingness to cooperate chased me out. Somehow I felt my work was done, and that I too was completely done in. It had come up so suddenly.

ATTEMPT to Articulate Sentiments

I marched off with only a vague inkling of where things were headed – I had news to share: a hatchling was born. Outside it was cloudy, windy, the workday half over. In all the commotion I had forgotten to eat lunch. I walked directly to the yellow garage and hoped that at Rainbow Pizza I would find the peace and quiet to record the incomprehensible feelings that had awakened in me when the hatchling emerged from the egg in the lab. Thus I would be able, I hoped, with the assistance of the written word, to comprehend my reaction. Recently I had read the following online:

'Accept your body. Write every day. Save your money. Call your mother. Limit your screen time.'

The unit's psychiatrists also encouraged us to keep diaries, as journalling helps regulate stress.

The girl sat behind the counter with her sketchbook open. I sat down at the same table Selma and I had dined at less than two weeks earlier. The waiter – from a name badge I read Vésteinn – laid out a glass, fresh water in a jug, and my yellow knitted hat. He had been freed from the bandages around his finger.

'Thank you,' I said and pointed to the hat, then to the finger.

'No problem,' he replied, and shook his index finger, then showed me the other for comparison. 'The finger smacked against a rock when I dove in for a swim, but it's coming along now.'

'Perhaps you know my sister?' I said and received an inkling that Æsa might practise ocean swimming constitutionally.

'Though I serve many, I recognise few,' he replied and wiped some fluff off the table. 'It is my lifelong goal to know few people and thus know better those whom I feign to know,' he said and retrieved some olive and chilli oils from nearby tables, looked at the girl – he wore eye frames that tried to conceal the eyes themselves – looked at me: 'What is your sister's name, may I ask?' His shirt was dove white, which is a pinker shade than crisp white, his apron college red, dark trousers and shoes. He shook his head, didn't know any Æsa.

'What about *her* mother?' I said, and the girl looked up.

'Lísa's mother is called Auðbjörg.'

'Does Auðbjörg maybe look a bit like me, or him?' I said, and showed Vésteinn a photograph of my brother Unnar, which I drew out of my wallet. He shook his head. Auðbjörg didn't have any siblings.

'Is she an orphan?' I said and meant Auðbjörg.

'No.'

Were Auðbjörg's parents definitely her biological parents? He pretended not to see my police badge.

'Auðbjörg is the spitting image of her parents,' Vésteinn replied.

'I'm allergic to healthy interaction,' I said and put my wallet back in my pocket. 'If you aspire to certainty and security you miss out on most things. And I no longer believe that conception takes place only during intercourse or artificial insemination between two or more people – things other than the technical aspects of reproduction must make a difference. What about day-to-day feelings, dreams, thoughts, diet, invisible forces? Are we alone in the universe? More things are probably invisible than we know. Why does conception sometimes succeed and oftentimes not? Even those who give up on intercourse and go to a clinic go there innumerable times and pay a fortune. What stubbornness is going on and what spiritual and unspiritual blockage is in place? Or is it stubbornnesses and blockages? Dogs and cats and tortoises show up in the house and suddenly – bang! bang bang! – *conception*! Do the creatures possess powers men don't? Why do the poor produce more offspring than the rich? No, Vésteinn, this is all rather mysterious and in any case risky and suspicious. And another question for the cosmos: What person in their right or wrong mind chooses to bequeath their burdens onto others – assuming traumas and disappointments can be inherited? No one can tell me that the heavenly or the earthly but mysterious creation of a child doesn't entail responsibility and empathy for the invisible – *hello!* – by the third birthday all respect for the unspeakable is gone. Might is cruelty, will is love. But it's not enough to love a child, you also need to care for it,' I gesticulated with my hands, 'and tell me this: How did this whole heap of *me* – if you can even call it that – come to be? From an invisible egg and cell?'

I hit myself in the face.

'Vésteinn, I'm telling you: We are sailing through a time in which the gods are allowing us to believe we can do anything and that we stand on the brink of inhuman power, but soon this period will pass like the wind changes direction and we will again be naked and defenceless. That will be their revenge.'

Vésteinn tapped the menu repeatedly against his chest.

'Yes, it could well be that something more lies behind any given act of conception; forces that, if not godly, are at least invisible,' he replied.

'In the old days,' I said, 'sex had a monopoly on conception and, as always, men of property organised reproduction as a matter of capital management, while the have-nots churned out children like factory parts, soldiers for wartime. It is more lucrative to make children transactionally and under legal contract than in a rush and carelessly. But in the end, all rivers run to the sea – all that fails, all that founders, and all the rest that succeeds, the chaotic as well as the orderly. Auðbjörg could be my sister, you my son, even if we were born the same year, the same day.' I hit the menu lightly against the table. 'But as long as there are people scraping by on low wages in order to prop up the astronomical wages of others who exploit them, as well as Earth herself, then no human being has the right to mourn their mother – yes please, I will order the world's finest anchovy pizza,' I added and threw my hand into the air.

While I waited for the world's best anchovy pizza I wrote in a diary that was later lost, so for the purposes of this recollection I rely on my gut – when the feeling awakens that I experienced at the birth of the hatchling, and which was reminiscent of expectation, apprehension, tension, longing, excitement, despair – *desire* – I try to approach her, this feeling, but she will not agree to any of these words, like a witness looking at an identity parade does not recognise any of the actors behind the one-way glass. She demands more specificity and sophistication in the word choice: 'The word that describes me is not among these words,' she, whom I call provisionally *desire*, complains, but she is absolutely not desire, and I, who attempt to describe her with more than one word, write:

My ears

      await

        screams and shouts from
the jungle, the fingers await an unshackled weed, the sense of
justice demands the roots from the molars that one after the other
were pulled from the jaws of our forefathers, the memory awaits

          the words of someone whom I thought I
knew and the hair or wig that I looked at one night.

   The palms salt
and salt and
salt
and salt and
salt the lips that I did not kiss because I despised kisses.

   Where is my sister, whose birthplace, and birthfact, is
unknown to me?

    Something
that I did not care for, that I could not identify or name, was
snatched from my hands and is not coming back.

Like the roof gutter that rusted apart and fell into my arms and which I carried out of the garden.

The hand that held together the broken coffee cup in the mornings disappeared.

And I, who wasn't capable of and refused longing, finally longed for atmosphere, moss, a blanket, and the cold on the other side of the blanket.

Of course I wasn't in my right mind.

A frank response by the feeling to the previous description: 'No, I'm sorry, Elísabet, you who out of generosity hosted me part of a day, thank you for the packaging, but this is not an accurate description of me, far from it.'

A writer, who was singled out in a case I later handled, said that the poems he wrote when he was young had been utter fabrications. But when he wrote the poems he felt they described real and unadorned feelings – *artless*. As long as the human race dwells in its thousand-year trauma – because even love and care entail oppression – it cannot be self-determining, said someone, maybe Grandma. I despise the adjective *unpretentious* less than the word *sincere*, but the meaning of each word is more ambiguous than the ambiguity of a single person, and words are the communal property of the masses. Why did I lose it when the hatchling broke free from the egg? I require an answer.

The Phone Call at Rainbow Pizza

As soon as Vésteinn placed the anchovy pizza on its ceramic dish on the table – ring – ring – ring – Lísa looked up. She still had hold of the red crayon. She listened in on the phone call while I pressed a fork repeatedly into the tabletop.

'I know where you are,' said Selma Mjöll on the other end of the line, and she cleared her throat. I didn't need to tell her that of course I knew that she knew, it was her job to know about the comings and goings of others. 'Elísabet Eva, you're fired.'

'Yes, but I already quit,' I replied, in accordance with the imagined truths of the moment.

'Then you forgot to leave a letter of resignation. You're fired and I'm glad to be rid of you, Elísabet, despite the utter nonsense known as fealty, which is just wheelings and dealings on the currency market. You don't know how to enjoy yourself. You're a human aberration. You're a disgusting person.'

'What?'

'Do I need to repeat myself?'

'No, thank you,' I replied, 'but is there some final thing I can do for you, before we part ways? I want to begin by thanking you for the collaboration, even though thankfulness is only a deposit into an account. Is there something that I can do for you personally to buy myself some peace – that is, if everything is transactional: a minimum reconciliation or at least a token of minimum reconciliation betwixt us?'

'Like what, you worthless piece of trash?'

'Do your tax return – have you handed it in? Knit you a jumper?'

After a moment of hesitation Selma answered:

'No thank you. Clean your conscience someplace other than on my person. We'll be watching you, as you know, you basket case.'

'Good to have one's suspicions confirmed. Thank you for firing me and sparing me the trouble.'

'Consider it my pleasure.'

'Will I get severance?'

'No, and you will return all your documents to the unit. Your computer's been wiped, your desk drawers emptied. I threw the photograph of your parents out the window.'

'I'll come by when I have a moment and sweep the broken glass off the pavement.'

'You'll come by at one o'clock tomorrow, get your crap and return the uniform.'

'Will do so with a mixed satisfaction but also thankfulness that I hope I won't need to pay for in my next life or harm myself on in this one.'

'Goodbye,' said Selma, and hung up the phone.

I smiled when I met Lísa's eye. The smile wanted to say:

Don't worry about a thing, dear Lísa, it's fine to be hung up on, especially if one is about to eat the world's best anchovy pizza, and in that regard you find yourself in the inner circle, being the daughter of Vésteinn. I grabbed the cutlery like a weapon. Lísa started colouring with the red crayon a picture of a crucifixion. Resolutely I cut the pizza into eight even sectors, free of doubt and what I had called previously, and provisionally, *desire*, but which was definitely not desire (as I've rehashed many times).

My servitude – which ten minutes earlier had been 100 per cent – had shrunk with the phone call by 25 per cent. Did desire belong only to the subjugated? Did a free person not desire? Had I asked Grandma, she would have smuggled in her reply propaganda about how I ought to live my life. My soul drew a breath in sync with my body, and vice versa. Breathe in. Breathe out. Breathe. In. Out. Breathe. In. Out. I would be free of another quarter if I could travel without surveillance – were I to turn off my phone and dodge the security cameras – beyond the city and deliver the news of the birth of the hatchling. I had forgotten to ask why I had been fired.

At a Crossroads

With my head held high I stood outside the yellow garage that housed Rainbow Pizza and looked in every direction. The weather was calm, the clouds were milk-white and heavy and did not remind me of the bosoms of female mammals. The wind that earlier whistled so spiritedly had been replaced by a fresh, gentle breeze. How quickly it had fled the scene. As in a movie or a dream – a page is turned, the wind is gone. With my dismissal I had gained roughly 25 per cent more freedom to do something out of my routine. According to my calculations, further freedom was hardly possible short of renouncing society outright.

But my savings accounts A and B resented the dismissal. Gently I closed the door to the room in my mind where A and B lived, not in the mood to listen to their lamentations.

Then it occurred to me to go beyond myself – to rip a hole in the so-called self-tent – and do some good, storm to the National Hospital and offer my assistance to the patients on the oncology ward. It also occurred to me to walk down to the square and make peace with Raccoon, buy him a birthday present.

Better late than never. If I didn't run into him I could entrust the gift to his associates. I searched my pockets for crumpled or smooth bills as well as loose change, to see whether I had something spare I could donate to the funds of the homeless, were I to pursue that course of action.

I had my full permission to just go home, hug Rex, mend the tent – isn't one meant to constantly be mending one's self-tent in one's spare time? – officiate a Yahtzee competition between Elísabet Eva 1 and Elísabet Eva 2, drink cacao.

As I grappled with a decision between such consequential choices, I felt compelled to move the wheels of commerce by taking the bus. A Special Unit task force had calculated the profit to the city were the unemployed to receive twenty to forty free weekday bus rides a month. Each step of the citizen added up, each occupied seat on the bus stimulated the staggering mechanism of a single society. The idea about the bus passes for the unemployed was being developed by the Ministry of Social Affairs and politicians debated whether those receiving unemployment benefits ought to be offered free round trips every workday or every other workday. Thus I thought it appropriate, while I made a decision about what to do with my life during the next few hours, to put my weight on the scales to champion, lubricate and subsidise the wheels of society, and walked tall and proud of my own volition this very moment – in this self-same moment that would disappear too soon, and therefore I enjoyed my pride as deeply as I could before it vanished into the abyss – to the next bus shelter.

The pace of walking dulled and calmed the mind. While

walking one distanced oneself from decisions and goals. While walking one didn't merge with anything; rather one got lost, fell out of society's records, since, as things stood, walking was still free of charge. As I strode towards the next bus shelter I got the idea, which I now had no hopes of realising, of introducing a tax on walks. That way they would acquire societal purpose. Moving at bus speed I would then achieve, or so I calculated in this excellent moment, the proper stimulation to make the best decision for my own good as well as the world's. I had read a study that suggested that the most successful decisions were made on the move, propelled either by mechanical power or that of horses – or else in the bathtub.

Next Stop of a Person Who Deep Down (Presumably) Did Not Choose to Extend Her Limited Freedom

The City Hospital loomed like a desert mirage on the rising slope of the city's oldest neighbourhood, coated in the crumbs of glimmering shells. When I walked through the brand-new surveillance gate, which smelled of paint and shimmered of gleamingly clean window glass, and into the hospital garden, having shown the guards my ID, which, as luck would have it, was still valid, the sun broke through the thicket of cloud and under its heavenly rays the building resembled a storybook castle.

It was not a pressing emergency that brought me to the hospital, as it was for most who moved through the area, but I wasn't ashamed of that and nor will I deny that my need to do good came hand in hand with a violent impulse and a pathological need for entertainment. The desire that refused to be called desire had perhaps morphed into a bitter impatience.

Outside the golden revolving doors a woman sat in a wheelchair and beside her stood a man on crutches. Between them was a tub full of cigarette stubs. They were smoking hand-rolled cigarettes. Their clothes were white – long undertrousers with a fly, and a shapeless top. Dignified, I bade them good afternoon.

'How is it going?' I asked with an acquired and feigned goodwill.

'Slowly but surely,' the woman replied with due suspicion.

'Same here,' replied the man in the same suspicious tone, as the infirm must be more on guard than everyone else.

'Do you require assistance? Shall I run out to the shop for you, buy lottery tickets?'

Their reaction might have been evidence of the veracity of my boss's claims about her former employee and associate.

'Just an idea,' I added. 'I'll be up on the chemo day unit if you need me, the name's Ástrós Sumarliðadóttir.'

As usual I introduced myself to the guards in the lobby as a representative of the government – my overcoat proved my raison d'être – didn't even need to show my badge. Evidently my dismissal had not yet been reported in the minutes that had passed between clearing the security gate out front and taking the lift upstairs.

Every quarter Selma and I would inspect the hospitals, since the Special Unit was tasked with monitoring whether the proper conditions were being maintained, for example that the selection of beverages in the vending machines remained limited, but we also kept an eye on various other things that I shouldn't mention, bound as I am to lifelong secrecy. Like whether everything wasn't definitely in a state of steady ruin, that the waiting lists grew longer and that patients lay in beds out in the hall, that strangers drew their last breaths communally in three- and five-person rooms and in the offices of doctors and secretaries, that their next of kin bumped into the cabin bags of other patients and into one another, that the dying words of strangers and the promises of friends and relatives hung in the air like mobiles and other decorations. That's socialism: Die together.

'It appears it will take more than a century of women's suffrage in this country before we'll see gowns sewn for patients,' Selma said once, after we had completed one of our surveys and were on our way down in the lift. 'Patients other than the ones in maternity wards and gynaecology wards do not have a sex,' she added, 'that's why I don't understand why they don't design sexless uniforms across the board rather than dressing everyone in men's underwear. When we gain power, Ella, we'll commission designs for the most beautiful patient-wear in the world. Do you think, though, Ella . . .' *Ella*? Was she confusing me for some *Ella*? '. . . that if low-waged and unskilled workers were better paid, people would stop bothering to get educated?'

'No.'

'But what if patient garb were beautiful – would people then flock to the National Hospital, the hotel of the poor, for free ministration?' she asked, and I answered that ugly patient attire did not get in the way of people getting sick and dying, as awful as it was for people to die badly dressed.

'You wouldn't get married or be confirmed in rags,' I added.

'Or be buried,' she added. 'Is it then possible that ugly clothes keep one alive?' she asked sagaciously.

'That could well be, Selma,' I replied sullenly, because I

wanted a hot dog from the hot dog stand out on the corner. That was where we usually headed after our visits.

'Would they recover faster or slower in beautiful clothes, or do the clothes not matter?' she said.

Still I did not know the answer and asked back whether people didn't fare better on higher salaries.

It would be impossible to know, she said and stuck her arm under mine and into my pocket.

'*I study your toes with a microscope but your soul with a telescope,*' said Selma, quoting a French author, and we laughed at the same time as the lift doors opened and we bade farewell to the guards in the lobby.

The orderlies in oncology received me with open arms. The head of department, Rakel Hauksdóttir, met me at her office and I explained over a cup of coffee – espresso from a vending machine – that the Special Unit was launching a humanitarian campaign this summer. That I was here to chat with patients currently undergoing chemotherapy and to inquire what might be done for them on a personal level during the treatment. Rakel applauded the campaign, offered up some purple confectionery, a gift from next of kin. We ate a few. Outside the window men in white overalls were dismantling scaffolding.

In the infusion room I sat down on a stool beside a woman sitting in a tall armchair with a built-in table. She wore blue clothes, a red scarf around her neck, had blue glasses, white shoes on her feet and a chestnut-brown wig on her head. The drugs were pumped into her right arm, which was tethered to a needle and a square package wrapped in tin foil resembling

a lunch box, which lay on the table attached to the chair. The
woman placed a green crossword book down on her lap. I introduced myself:

'My name is Ástrós and it is my job to bring people hope.'

My interlocutor's name was Lilja Ósk.

'How is the treatment going, Lilja Ósk?'

'So-so – but tell me, what did you say you did again, dear?'

'Work for the city, we offer people hope.'

'How do you do that? By lying to me?' she said and fixed the
crooked wig that I had pointed out was askew.

'The margins between deception, falsehood, fantasy and
truth are rather muddled and become ever more muddled and
confusing with increased technological advancements, which,
indeed, are built on the deceptions of physics,' I replied. 'But we
at the Ministry of Hope specialise in humanitarian aid and stir
it all together into a potion – fantasy, truth, and all that – and
water people with it.'

Lilja Ósk had trouble righting her wig.

'Allow me,' I said and fixed the wig. 'There.'

'You are not convincing in your job though you are good at
righting wigs. Thank you, Ástrós.'

'It was my pleasure. Do you want to send me out to the
shop? Do you need some crisps? Something more concrete than
hope?'

'I don't need anything, thank you,' Lilja Ósk replied.

I fetched a handkerchief from my pocket and gave it to Lilja
Ósk, who inspected the embroidered rose like a professional
seamstress.

'I think you are a clown,' she said, laughed, and returned the kerchief. 'And if you are a clown you should be entertaining in nursery schools instead.'

'Five-year-olds laugh five hundred times a day,' I began my speech, 'a twenty-year-old woman twenty times, a thirty-year-old ten times, a forty-year-old once a day, a fifty-year-old every third day, a sixty-year-old every half year, a seventy-year-old every two years,' I said, and rose from the stool, fetched from my pocket a recorder flute played a piece of a children's rhyme by a Hungarian composer, did a little dance, bowed, and walked

slantwise

across the floor to a man who opened his eyes when I sat down on the stool beside his chair. He was bald with a raven nose, clad in grey clothes, yellow socks and raffia shoes. In dreamworlds I was rarely or even never – but I can't say for certain – guilty of violence or impoliteness and had never committed murder in a dream, if I remember correctly. I waited patiently for the grey-clad man to initiate the conversation, in this way I hoped to prove to no one but myself my civility in waking life. After a long silence he reached for a glass of orange juice on the table and brought it to his lips.

'Orange juice exacerbates the nausea brought about by the medication,' I said and tore the glass from him when he had drunk a bird sip – I left the room, came back in – 'but apple juice calms nausea,' I added like an advertisement and placed the glass on the table. He drank the apple juice.

'There,' I said and helped him place the glass back on the table, 'it will be all right and even if it won't be all right, then that's all right too – suffering is not always the worst option,' I added, and when I realised what I had just said I apologised. A strange air follows when one offers an apology to a man who silently pays such close attention to everything.

'I apologise,' I repeated and bowed, 'for the crowding, the impoliteness, the impingement, the coercion,' and played the ditty again on the flute – I completely refused to give up, I was sick and tired of suffering defeat in my interactions with animals and men; I bowed again and said:

'This is a riddle. Are you ready? Once a woman walked along a very long road on a rather hot day and held a box filled with blueberries. The road was so long and the day so hot that her hand got tired from holding the box and the woman stuck the blueberries into her shirt pocket. What color was the shirt?'

'White,' replied the man, and cleared his throat.

'Right answer,' I replied and bowed, played the ditty a third time, walked backwards out of the infusion room – or the confusion room, as some imbecilic jokers liked to call it – let the handkerchief fall on the open spread of the crossword book that lay in the lap of the woman who slept. I had manifested the words of my boss: *human aberration*.

As I headed down a long hallway my phone rang in my coat pocket. I didn't recognise the number but I did recognise my colleagues who were walking in my direction – Axel and Lóa – accompanied by two guards in navy-blue jumpers, Rakel the department head, and an unknown nurse. Lóa apologized after we greeted one another:

'We're sorry about this, Elísabet,' she added and looked doleful.

'Very sorry,' her fiancé emphasised.

'According to orders from our superiors we have to sedate you,' Lóa concluded and pointed to the nurse, who was marked with the name Barði on a blue badge alongside a photograph.

'Wouldn't it be more comfortable to sedate me in the privacy of a room?' I asked Rakel, who turned around and pointed to a door with a number that I didn't care to see. The flock followed me in. I laid my coat neatly at the foot of the bed, though neither it nor the surroundings deserved my care, lay down on the bed, and directed my question to Axel and Lóa: 'Well, comrades, how will we go about washing our hands of it all?'

'Don't make this more difficult than it already is,' Lóa implored and stuck a finger in her dimple.

'Why not?' I said. 'Why do we always have to spare ourselves the effort?'

'Because it's hard enough as it is,' Axel replied.

My eyes followed the faces of these people, unknown and known, who arranged themselves around the bed. A white sun lit up the white surfaces of the room but I felt it did not illuminate the people.

'We who are specially trained to endure difficulty should never shy away from it,' I couldn't be bothered to reply, and in any case I must have misunderstood something fundamental in the basic training, or misunderstood something else, anything, everything.

My eyes admired the fire-red hair of Barði, who calmly dressed his hands in blue gloves.

'Despite everything and everything we are friends,' said Axel, and he and Lóa averted their eyes.

'Yes,' I replied and thought of the electric chair, that well-known execution tool used for the first time in New York City in the year 1890, and fell asleep as soon as Barði pressed down the syringe's piston, injected me with drugs.

Next Stop: Hall of Mirrors

I dreamed that the dandruff in my hair was shards of glass. I dreamed that the dandruff was snowflakes. That it was full stops and semicolons. I shivered from cold and awoke, looked into a face that I recognised as possibly my own, turned onto my other side, onto my back, discerned an indistinct mass in the air. Nothing in the cell shielded me from the mirror image besides my short-sightedness and the bed, which was a mattress on a steel bench that hung from a chain in the ceiling. Through some sly feat of engineering a coldness slid its way through the mirrors. I had last seen myself in a mirror when I was seventeen years old and getting undressed in Grandma's bedroom while the water bellowed into the bathtub on the other side of the wall. Then I folded the clothes and laid them on the bed, which truly deserved to be treated beautifully. Grandma made the bed at the stroke of seven each morning. Absent-mindedly on my way to the bathroom I had caught sight of myself in the long mirror behind the door.

The distance between body and reflection is equal to the distance between body and language, someone wrote – it could be compared to a ravine that engulfs you, or a desert that dries you out if you dare to venture in. Like the poet who opposed the telescope when it came to market, or the singers who protested the footsteps on the moon, I was the adversary of mirrors.

'Time stops while you look at yourself in a mirror,' said the mirror in Grandma's bedroom. 'And you will owe time that time forever.'

'How so?'

'Surely you understand the meaning,' replied the mirror. 'People don't rob only time of their reflection while they gawp, but also the sky and water – avert your eyes!'

Still I averted my eyes.

In the cell it was indestructibly cold. Under the wool blanket, which prickled and was emblazoned with the crest of the state, I touched my body and felt I was the carriages of a stalled train. I recognised the underwear, however, and despised the individual who, on salary, had undressed me, and would have despised him even if he was not. I waited calmly while the carriages loosened from their tracks, rose to my feet, drained and fierce, defeated and aching, fumbled along the mirror floor, my feet locked together, searched for my glasses, my clothes, socks – dispossessed of my coat – wrapped the scratchy woollen blanket tighter around me.

A year earlier a committee of three gentlemen pensioners had gone to take a course with the ministry's partners in the US on the solitary confinement of inmates. They had not yet delivered a lecture about the trip for staff at the ministry, as was the custom when people attended courses abroad. Nowhere had I read anything about cells lined with mirrors, and I applauded the ingenuity. Was I a guinea pig? Why wouldn't I be able to endure that? In basic training I was coached in how to endure quarantine without injury, using the following tactics:

Letter writing (with or without stationery); prayer; meditation; the recital of poems: poems about animals, others about time; narration of Buddhist teachings; gymnastics drills and stretches; song; deliberate maintenance of cognitive connections to friends and family; wariness of deception, delusion and fantasy.

That is: One places oneself into preservation like food into the freezer.

I ripped a strip of fabric from my nightshirt and tied it over my eyes with a view to preserving my ignorance of my mirror image, and sang to myself, without a particular melody, a poem about animals:

> And nearly had I lost my wits
> and still my sense is fazed –
> should faerie folk turn foe, your soul
> shall not soon be saved.
> *Leave all birds be,*
> *leave all birds be! in the spring.*

The cell went dark. I lay down in bed and imagined that Rex lay with me under the blanket, fell asleep and dreamed that I was lying on a larger mattress alongside more dogs, while children and puppies searched in containers and cupboards for food that was nowhere to be found. I hurried myself to wake up and free Rex from the captivity of the dream and reassumed the vessel that shivered with cold.

Attack

A ragged being lay on top of me and crushed me, tore off my blindfold and put me in a stranglehold. In the half-light I discerned the stare of a promising murderer, an eager twinkle that could be described as hotly passionate, because it was reminiscent of a bonfire, but the grimace foamed with ice-cold delight. It must be fun to kill, I thought. Then my breathing became severely restricted, I stopped being able to cough but raised my torso up quickly causing the human to roll out of the bed. I worried that it had harmed itself in the fall so I clambered to my feet and poked its shoulder, but at that the figure jumped to its feet and felled me. I crashed to the floor, it threw itself on top of me and started to strangle me, screaming:

'What is wrong?'

A beautiful question, were a mother to calmly ask it of her child who is crying for unknown reasons. I couldn't decide whether I ought to root for myself or this cursed being, plagued as I was by a pathological need to actively side with my enemies. How do you answer a dangerous lunatic?

'Nothing is wrong,' I replied, struggling for breath.

'Of course there's something wrong, of course there's something *wrong*, old maid, something is WRONG, something is bloody WRONG –'

'No, nothing, unless you plan to murder me.'

'Yes!' it screamed so my ears echoed, 'I *a m h e r e* to fry your brain.'

It raised its fist in the air and I closed my eyes, awaited the blow: would my jaw break? – would I lose a tooth, teeth? – would the guards answer the bell right away or wait until I had bled out? A moment passed and a heavy tear fell onto my face. Ew –

'What is wrong?'

It was my turn to ask. I was unable to wipe my face since the being still had my arms pinned.

'Nothing,' it replied and towered over me, seemed to be about to slobber into my face. 'Kiss me,' it said and stroked my wet cheek, brushed my hair from my face like a mother might. That was too much for me. I lost all the strength in my body as it bent down and kissed me. I didn't want this. I didn't want this at all. I didn't want to be a person. This was beyond all laws, beyond crime, beyond innocence, beyond the neutrality that guided my life. Now I would never regain my neutrality. The being brushed the hair from my face. Like a mother.

'Don't say that I'm a person and have needs like everyone else,' I begged, and spat out gravel.

'I wasn't going to say anything,' replied the being, 'I was just going to brush the hair from your face and take a better look at you.'

It fetched some gravel from its own mouth.

'Don't look at me,' I said and recoiled from the being, who had loosened its grip during its fondling. I stood up. Then it jumped maniacally to its feet and, rather than attacking me, struck the walls with such force that the mirrors broke.

'You'll hurt yourself,' I said calmly to the frenzied guest. 'Though I am thankful to you for breaking the mirrors, you're going to hurt yourself.'

Then it turned around and I recognised the lunatic who once again attacked me and put me in a stranglehold.

'Will you please not kill me,' I said to myself. I don't remember anything after that.

Invigilation

After an indeterminate sleep – in the hall of mirrors both sleep and waking became indeterminate, likewise thoughts, even ordinary words – I heard through my half sleep the sound of a page being turned. It had warmed up a bit. Under the blanket I found my hands wrapped in bandages, my face covered with plasters, and the smell of blood and iodine. Another page was turned. I peeked out from under the blanket and could vaguely make out a stooped person sitting with their legs crossed on a stool beneath the bench, wearing jeans and an operating-room-green T-shirt, and reading a book. I listened for a long time to the even breathing. Another page was turned. I asked what they were reading. The person looked up.

'The book is not about anything. My name is Jakob by the way, but the book doesn't have a name,' the person replied and waved the book. The jacket showed an orange sun on a purple background. I was going to introduce myself when Jakob added: 'I found it by chance at the library and am reading it for the third time, I recommend it,' Jakob said and knocked on the book.

'Does nothing happen, then?'

'Oh yes, a lot happens, but there's no single prevailing topic, as in: This book is about cruelty, about self-perception, power, powerlessness.' Jakob knocked on the book. 'If everything is fine and dandy in one's life then it isn't about anything; if something goes wrong, then life acquires a genre. If good fortune follows me, then my life isn't about happiness per se, and if the book is about happiness, it's a self-help book – I've had enough of those for now,' Jakob knocked on the book, 'and anyway it's high time I acted on the advice I've read. In the meantime I'm reading a book about nothing, the effect of which is similar to that of wandering about town. Aren't you especially fond of roaming about town?'

'Yes, very much so,' I replied.

'Ah, I do too little of that, can't get myself out of the house unless I know where I'm headed. At most I roam about with the kids on Saturdays, but that's more of a jaunt.'

'My wandering always ends in order and routine,' I replied.

'Yes, that can happen,' replied Jakob. 'Best not to roam too much so the roaming stays as roaming and doesn't become an addiction, because then it loses its meaning. Addiction is liberation from disorder.'

Jakob knocked on the book.

'A book that isn't about anything never disappoints you. Books that search for a conclusion and closure are at risk of disappointing their readers. Conclusions dampen the impulse to innovate and to imagine.'

Jakob knocked on the book.

'Like in most books there are of course characters and set-
tings.' Jakob leafed quickly through the book. 'Now I am reading the chapter where Diana and Janus meet in a beautiful blue
valley and become friends – not lovers, there is no love in the
book. These dear friends are locked up in separate houses in
a most beautiful valley, with a fence between them, while they
design and develop a video game that has the effect of instilling
in its players a longing to commit suicide.'

'What on earth?'

'Yes,' replied Jakob, 'indeed. As soon as they have finished
developing the game they are released from the dale and can
go home. One person's freedom at the price of another's death.'

I was going to ask whether the book had the same effect as
the video game but the stool was empty. It was an advertisement. I found my blindfold under the pillow and put it on, got
up, was going to pee, call the guards, ask for water. The lights
went out again.

– ! –

I awoke often to a glaring brightness. Then the brightness faded, grew dim, and I awoke to a deep darkness whose duration I struggled to measure, until the lights came on again. So it went on, alternating at irregular time intervals. I thought it unlikely that the light tampering was meant to teach me to reconcile with the mirror image, that the mirror image was the core that the darkness destroyed with the help of self-hatred, and that it would come to light whether I could be at peace with myself or become completely sick of myself. Or which phobia spared me less: that of the darkness or of my reflection. Of course I knew that mental conditioning did not take place in a prison cell, but one could hope.

Gradually it got warmer in the cell while my underwear and bandages greyed, my hair and nails grew, and my wounds, were they left in peace, healed. I meditated, sang, recited poems about animals and time, told myself stories, tired myself out with riddles, wrote Rex letters, wrote Rex letters, wrote to my friend:

'Dear Rex, I sit in a hall of mirrors and my thoughts dwell

with you but still can't get a foothold or find peace of mind anywhere.'

I did stretches, hopped around in circles, said my prayers until the prayers attacked me in the dark with bared teeth and asked me unkindly to return the gifts that life had given me, directly or indirectly, in whatever form, each and every gift. When the guards carried in the orange food trays I hid myself completely under the blanket so I couldn't be seen at all, and in between I disappeared into Rex – poor Rex having to house me – and fell asleep.

In my meditations I mounted a winged steed that whisked me away towards the free state where men laugh instead of crying, but the distance got ever longer and longer while I hurtled at the speed of light away from my point of departure. I picked the plasters off my face, repeatedly tore open my wounds and scratched myself until I bled, sucked and licked the blood and chewed the cud, double-digested myself. I probably counted incorrectly sixteen food trays with breakfast, twelve with lunch, eleven with dinner, then someone threw in through the hatch a pair of laceless trainers and a blue one-piece that smelled of developing liquid. I put on the clothes and with great effort and dexterity the shoes, waited a few moments for the arrival of two guards, who handcuffed me and let me out. Then I pulled down my blindfold with the help of one of the guards and recognised the light-green hallway and the interrogation room, to which I was led. After a few more moments Helgi Björn Björnsson entered without using a key – ! –

(– ! – marks the moment one is free but doesn't know it.)

I knew immediately that Selma Mjöll was not watching behind the one-way glass when Helgi Björn sat down without taking off his jacket. Around Selma, Helgi only ever wore a shirt, or so my female colleagues, enthusiasts about men's waists, had noted. He bid me good afternoon.

'Good afternoon,' I replied, disoriented.

'Rósa does not send Frankó her regards.'

'Frankó does not send Rósa her regards.'

From his pocket he drew a folded sheet of paper. He handed me my glasses, adjusted his own on his nose while I adjusted mine, and read the heading on the sheet of paper: *Superseding Contract*.

'We decided to forgive you,' he said and laid one of his hands – long fingers, wedding ring – on the table, the other on his thigh.

'Forgive me for what?'

'Gross negligence. You really crossed the line this time.'

'You could have drawn the line more clearly,' I replied, and read the subheading: *Promotion, terms of employment*.

'Maybe you have a point there but you're splitting hairs, Elísabet Eva. Little Selene has smashed all attendance records at the City Zoo. People come from all over to see a creature that symbolises the union of animal and man, nature and civilisation. The zoo is booked up two years in advance. All thanks to a shipment addressed to you, Elísabet.'

I barely missed anything from the world of humans, trained as I was to resist the hegemony of feelings.

'How are things with Rósa and Venus?' asked Frankó.

His eyelids quivered so beautifully that I wanted to give Venus a gift: an espresso pot; a jar of honey from the abbey we visited after the conference in Vienna on techniques for disseminating propaganda; chocolates handmade by the state's former football coach and current confectionery master and head of the civil liberties union; a pan to roast coffee beans on; my parents' stamp collection; a custom-made bedding set; a camping blanket – the ideas for gifts floated like billboard ads through my mind while Venus's eyelids quivered. Then he drew a deep breath in the same way Selma and I drew breaths in the middle of a conversation, she first, then me, or the other way around, and wrote in a notebook in a secret code that only Frankó, Rósa and Venus could read and that had taken them several weeks to develop and perfect and that my parents would probably have been interested in studying:

To Frankó's happiness and pleasure, Venus has not separated from D. A certain someone does not want to get engaged to V.

In the secret language I scrawled, with my wrists locked together and my hands wrapped in bandages such that my handwriting was not at its very best, in his notebook:

Frankó is above all feelings, but what does D want?

He scribbled over the sentences and tucked the notebook into his inner pocket.

'What's the difference between a toy and a lab rat?' I asked and could hear that I sounded as feeble as a dame who can't fathom her constriction and, what's more, is bound with chains that are alternately visible and invisible, depending on the circumstances, as they say. Then Helgi looked rather beautifully into my eyes:

'Maybe nothing, and maybe that the toy doesn't receive a wage.'

He drummed his fingers on the table for a few seconds.

'Not a trace has been found of the swan stock, little Selene's aunts, by the green lake or in its vicinity. We've utilised traditional and non-traditional methods in the search, even recruited a medium. I don't know the names of all the tracking devices that have been used – the zoologists came, specialists in excrement, archaeologists, botanists, entomologists, countless samples were taken and sent to Sweden. Not a single dropping or drop of spit, but we aren't ruling anything out. How did this egg come to be?'

They must have had me down as a certifiable chocolate eclair, entitled to special treatment, since I got away with just shrugging my shoulders.

'We're holding on to the one per cent chance that something will be found. It would be wonderful if Selene gained a companion of her kind, both for her sake and that of the future, for the country and the children of this country. We must expand the zoo because of the record attendance and make sure the numbers never, ever decline. We presume you have the confidence of these creatures who are nowhere to be found except in your head and in the egg sent to the Special Unit. It's unnecessary to rehash that whole story.'

'The swanfolk's measuring devices must be more precise and sensitive than ours,' I replied, but Helgi Björn stood up, kneeled at my feet and removed the iron chains from my ankles. I didn't spit on the back of his neck. Nor did I stroke his hair, which smelled of . . . chamomile? He took from his pocket an electronic tag and snapped it around my right ankle, stood up, loosened my handcuffs, opened the unlocked door, neither said goodbye nor closed the door behind him.

The contract lay on the table. The first paragraph described how I would lead an investigation into the sexual behaviour of young women. I could choose two assistants, and I decided immediately on Axel and Lóa. In the paragraph's footnote describing the pay rise and benefits it stated that my pay would be docked to cover the cost of repairing the mirrors I broke, and cited an article of a law regarding vandalism of state property. Savings account A whispered to savings account B something I did not care to hear. I walked out and followed green exit signs down long narrow passageways up onto the ground floor.

In the twilit lobby there still sounded the echo of Helgi Björn's footsteps. The sky-high walls gleamed in the light cast by diamond-shaped lamps made of gold and heavenshells, the rays of light were thrown in diamond-shaped streaks up the mirror-polished wood panelling. My shadow ran frightened circles around me like a lifebuoy, but no sound came from my antlike footsteps. From the gate Jónatan followed me with his eyes. I bade him good evening, asked after Adda. No reply. How Burkni was getting on with his studies, Sóley with her pregnancy. Whether the golden plover had arrived out east, the leaf buds blossomed. How many oranges he had eaten today.

'Seven.'

'Seven,' I repeated, and took my leave.

Outside, the evening was getting on but it was not yet completely dark. In the air I detected a faint scent of spring. I followed the coastline home in rain that tried its best to go undetected as rain, and oh how I understood its intent: one chooses to conceal oneself, one must conceal oneself. For all of eternity humankind would misunderstand the phenomena of integrity and honesty – thought I, who didn't know what the word *truth* meant.

Rex was nowhere to be seen around the bus stop. Perhaps he had forgotten himself while sorting the undated letters from the prison cell. Would he sort them on a scale of agitation (-10) to calmness (+10)?

At home my papers and files had all been ransacked, pink stationery torn apart, books tipped out of the shelves, cutlery from the drawers, the pantry rummaged. No calendar. No phone. I couldn't find the television remote anywhere, nor the cord for the red radio, which was meant to stand in the kitchen window but lay instead on the floor. I opened the window. The night walked in.

On a hook out in the hall hung my overcoat, my pride and distinguishing feature, in a dry-cleaning bag, together with my bag, the blue-grey one. The boots belonging to Mum, Æsa, or Grandma had been rinsed. In the pocket of the coat I found my yellow knitted hat; my notebook was gone, but legally speaking it could be said to be the property of my employer. I listened to the music of a French composer, lowered myself into a pine-needle bath, unwrapped the bandages from my hands. Some-one had placed chamomile shampoo and honey soap on the edge of the tub.

AT THE WATER

Undated

Late Supper Following
Solitary Confinement

To my mind it was a tremendous sacrifice to give myself to the state in exchange for freedom amounting to a hundred-kilometer radius. In a pan I fried sausages that I found in the fridge. Whoever had put the sausages there clearly had no intention of poisoning me before I had filed my final report on the local stand-up scene of winter 20XX–20XX, investigated and filed a report on the sexual conduct of young women, and fished up for the City Zoo at least one more egg containing a nestling, preferably male, of the kind half swan and half human. I mashed boiled potatoes with a potato masher from Grandma's collection, fetched from the pantry a jar of mustard, sat down to eat at the red kitchen table my brother had given me for my birthday, tucked a napkin into my collar and looked up under the chandelier, at which point God Almighty called upon me:

EARTHLY DAUGHTER, ELÍSABET EVA, DAUGHTER OF UNNUR AND RÚNAR.

Present, I replied in soldierly fashion.

YOU HAVE BEEN STATIONED HERE IN ORDER TO IN-

VESTIGATE THE WORLD OF MAN, YOUR REPORT I WILL
READ OFF YOUR ORGANS AND YOUR HEARTBEAT, THE
SCARS ON YOUR LIVER, THE DENTS IN YOUR CEREBRAL
HEMISPHERE, THE STATE OF YOUR TEETH AND GUMS,
YOUR EYES AND EARS, YOUR UTERUS, YOUR COLON.

I brought my hands together.

Thank you, my lord, I shall try to bear witness to mankind
on Earth impartially and without greed, opportunism, or self-
interest.

THANK YOU, DAUGHTER.

Thank you, eternal father.

YOU ARE NOT MY FAVOURITE DAUGHTER, BUT I CARE
FOR YOU SINCERELY AND WITHOUT AFFECTATION – THAT
IS TO SAY, IN GOOD FAITH. I DO NOT PRETEND TO LOVE
YOU, BECAUSE I DO NOT NEED TO PRETEND, BECAUSE I
OWN THE ENTIRE WORLD. HAD I NOTHING, I MIGHT PRE-
TEND TO LOVE IN ORDER TO COUNTERVAIL THE LACK. IS
THAT NOT BOTH CORRECT AND LOGICAL?

Yes, thank you, dear father. What is the meaning of all of this,
by the way, darling father?

UNLIKE MANKIND I DO NOT NEED TO PRETEND TO
LOVE IN ORDER TO CONCEAL SOME OTHER LACK AND
TO CONCEAL THE LOVELESSNESS ITSELF – IF I AM A
LOVELESS GOD, THEN THAT'S JUST HOW IT IS. BUT WHAT
DO YOU THINK, MY DEAR DAUGHTER? IS YOUR FATHER
BEREFT OF LOVE?

No, you are love itself, heavenly father, without you there
would be nothing.

CORRECT ANSWER – I SWEAR IT, AND I MAY SWEAR ALL THAT IT OCCURS TO ME TO SWEAR. YOUR FATHER TRUSTS IN YOUR FALLIBILITY TO DO GOOD DEEDS AND DOES NOT CARE IF YOU BETRAY HIS TRUST, IT IS HUMAN TO ERR. I WISH I WERE ABLE TO EXPERIENCE FALLIBILITY LIKE A PERSON EXPERIENCES IMPERFECTION. SOMETIMES I TRY AND FAIL HUMANKIND, AND YOU KNOW WHAT, IT CHANGES NOTHING ABOUT MY SENTIMENTS, WHICH ARE NONE. YOU ALL STOPPED DISAPPOINTING ME A LONG TIME AGO, LIKEWISE MAKING ME PROUD. IS THAT GOOD OR BAD, DAUGHTER?

Dear father, I think that is both good and bad.

OH, DAUGHTER, CHOOSE ONE WAY OR THE OTHER.

(I rolled my eyes in my head while I made a decision about whether to choose an honest answer or an appropriate one.)

Good.

ACH, I DON'T WANT TO BE ON THE SIDE OF GOOD.

Bad.

THANK YOU.

Don't mention it. But perhaps tell me one thing, heavenly father. My colleague read something in an old text, which has since been lost to the world, about the gods – that you had all abandoned the planet a long time ago, though the goddesses not right away. You speak as if you are one man, or perhaps more precisely one thing, one power. Where have your brothers and sisters got to, may I ask?

MY DEAR DAUGHTER, I CANNOT BE EXPECTED TO ANSWER SUCH BLASPHEMY.

Why not? Are you the only one left?

AM I THE ONLY ONE LEFT?

What happened? Did you kill the goddesses? Did they kill themselves? You can tell me, because I judge no one. I received first-class training in the academy in never assuming a judgemental attitude.

DAUGHTER, I GAVE YOU ALL EVERYTHING, BUT YOU TOOK EVEN MORE, AND IF I AM NOT TO BE DONE AWAY WITH I MUST FIRST AND FOREMOST PROTECT MYSELF. MY FREEDOM IS AT STAKE. IF I AM NOT CAREFUL YOU WILL COLONISE ME COMPLETELY, AND IT'S BAD ENOUGH AS IT IS –

God. Don't go yet, God.

I MUST GO, DAUGHTER. I'VE HAD ENOUGH OF THIS, I AM BORED UP HERE IN THIS UGLY CHANDELIER.

But God almighty, perhaps the goddesses can help you?

I LIED EARLIER. BUT THE THING IS, DAUGHTER, I AM ALLOWED TO LIE, BECAUSE IF I DON'T LIE, THE LIE WILL DISAPPEAR FROM THE WORLD AND NO ONE WANTS THAT, SO I LIED: I SOMETIMES ADMIRE YOU HUMANS AND WILL SIT DOWN ON A GOOD LOOKOUT POINT TO ADMIRE YOU BETTER AND BE FILLED WITH AN ENDLESS FATHERLY PRIDE WHEN I OBSERVE THE CARGO BEING MOVED AROUND THE ENORMOUS WATERFRONT LOADING DOCKS. THE ORGANISATION IS EXCEPTIONAL, ALL THAT SECURITY AND SURVEILLANCE. IT WOULD NEVER HAVE OCCURRED TO ME TO BUILD A CARGO LORRY. OF COURSE I HAD THE IDEA FOR THE FIRST CARGO SHIP,

BUT I WOULD NEVER HAVE BEEN ABLE TO INVENT THE
SHIPPING CONTAINER. OR ALL THAT COMPLICATED
ORGANISATION OF TRANSPORT. SOMETIMES I REACH
MY HAND OUT TOWARDS A SAILING SHIP ON A FAIR
SUMMER EVENING – I AM TEMPTED TO PICK IT UP OUT
OF THE OCEAN AND TAKE A CLOSER LOOK. OR GRAB
TRAINS ON THE MOVE, OR PLANES FROM THE AIR. YOU
EXCEEDED MY WILDEST EXPECTATIONS, WHICH WERE
NONE. I GAVE YOU EVERYTHING BECAUSE I WAS WOR-
RIED FOR YOU, POWERLESS CREATURES WITH DELICATE
TEMPERAMENTS WHO SING BEAUTIFULLY IN THE EVE-
NINGS AND AT NIGHT AND WHO CRY IN INSCRUTA-
BLE PAIN, WHICH IS AT ONCE HEAVENLY AND EARTHLY
AND WORTHLESS. I AM ROOTING FOR YOU ALL, EACH
AND EVERY ONE OF YOU – ACH, WHAT DO YOU THINK I
SHOULD DO, DAUGHTER, IN THIS MOMENT THAT IS AL-
READY SLIPPING AWAY FROM US, LAUGH OR CRY? I DON'T
WANT TO SOUND LIKE A DAME. I FEEL EMPTY-HANDED
AND STRANGE –

And so the heavenly touch faded as quietly as footprints in
the sand. I cut a sausage into bits like I was holding a saw,
and as I put a piece into my mouth I began, completely involuntarily, to think about the free state – in this way sausages liberate the mind from its shackles – about how Grandma
and I would have got on and enjoyed ourselves there. Would
we have been happier heading out to pick the berries from the
trees, or would we have been equally happy picking berries
from the trees there, as in this land, or in utopia? Would we

have been calmer or more worked up as we pulled the carrots from the ground with the broadfork, or been equally calm and equally worked up in all three lands? Would we have eaten fresh salad at lunch, laughing? Does one laugh more or less in a free state? What is a free state, anyway? In what kind of state do I live? How do they laugh in a totalitarian state? I cut the sausage into bits and imagined that the fork was the size of a muddy broadfork.

Riddle
(this might be a loathsome digression):

Dearest reader, a handbook for writers warns against the phenomena *author surrogacy* and *digression*. In this chapter the surrogate steps up and isn't exactly trying to hide. Dearest reader. What would you think about if you were sitting on the bench outside the room with the execution chair, the guard just moments away from fetching you? Take some time to think it over before you read my answer and try to utilise the techniques of meditation: I sit on a bench outside the room with the execution chair, within a few minutes – an enormous clock on the tall, narrow wall doesn't just resemble a jaw, it *is* a jaw – an executioner and guards will fetch me. What do I think about? Do me a favour and don't look at my answer on the next page right away. If you follow my instructions you may never repeat the game.

One plays for time if one can't bring oneself
to say goodbye. I am (not) a robot.

Formal Beginning of a Masquerade

Security cameras hung under the roof gutters of my house, each in its own corner. I had reclaimed the overcoat, the taupe trench: the shared property of me and the state – my self-image, my identity. I was myself again. A citizen of a community. Without my coat I lost my bearings. At two after midnight I smelled of the treasured soaps, my hair and clothes clean: I had lived to witness my own resurrection. After so many days of squalor under the artificial lights, I hadn't regained my sense of time just yet. I felt it was day when it was night. The near future would entail the following:

I would march on destiny, walk down to the lake, meet the swandames, inform them of the birth of Selene, daughter of Álfrún Perla and Earl Prince Karl, and of her success in the City Zoo. We would sit down to negotiate.

The swanfolk would (hopefully) hand over another egg on the condition that I take it somewhere warm and safe. They wouldn't trust me fully and would know better than I whose puppet I was pretending not to be. I would try to convince them otherwise, that I had a mind to betray my superiors, the state, and the Special Unit, or rather *play* them.

But my superiors would never be content with just one egg, they'd want more and more, and not rest until they had harvested everything. In my childish naïveté I would believe I had the power to persuade my wards, find them shelter that secured their freedom and well-being, and to betray my employer. God didn't give a shit – when it came to financial gain, the state exceeded God.

I did not have the power to strike a deal with the swanfolk and betray my superiors, yet had trouble believing in anything but my own (super)strength. Until I had failed completely, I would continue to believe I could heroically change the world without sacrificing my life. In this fantasy I would carry on working for the Special Unit, would finish the report on stand-up comedy, submit it to the minister of the interior, start and finish an investigation into the sexual conduct of young women, write and submit a report to the minister of equality. Normal days would follow as well as happy moments in the kitchenette with my colleagues, the swandames and their princes safely sheltered where no one could find them; I would take the secret to my grave. But the story would not go that way. A masquerade commenced.

All rivers run to the sea, and I who could neither determine nor steer their course didn't recognise the riverbeds. I would lose. The swanfolk would lose. My superiors would lose, though decades or even centuries would pass before their loss became apparent. Only their successors would bear witness to the defeat, albeit without exactly being aware of it as such – foo tsteps – stories – traces – all fully disappeared.

Like the lead actor in a play, I bowed for the cameras. No one saw Rex, who thanked me for the letters from my jail cell by licking my boots and sniffing out the smell of the honey, the chamomile soap, the sausages and the cedarwood oil.

Song

On my walk down to the water my self disappeared into an inscrutable happiness. Day-to-day I felt neither good nor bad. I forgot my objectives; forgot who my masters were – my bank account, God, the minister of the interior, myself, the swanfolk; forgot who had ownership of me and my coat and the camera that I always forgot to use. I sat down on the green bench, looked out over the green lake, up at the fire-blue sky whose transition from night to day would be effortless, enjoyed my breath, breathing air into my lungs and then returning it changed. My custodians: heaven and earth. The water: my siblings. The bushes: my cousins, the leaf buds their offspring. I didn't know that I didn't matter and I didn't know that I mattered and I knew that I mattered and knew that I didn't matter. Without stirring a hair on my head the creatures had surrounded me, humans on swan plinths, their fins submerged in the tall grass. The swanfolk swayed and sang:

> *we wish you well and we wish you ill*
> *we wish you well and we wish you ill*
> *m-m-m-m-m-m-m*

———

we wish for you everything and we wish you nothing
m-m-m-m-m-m-m swans and humans
you are us and we are you and something and nothing and everything
m-m-m-m-m-m-m swans and humans

———

Blíng is cold and Kornlilja is anguished, for the hatchling disappeared
Ástríður is hungry and our leader can't remember her name
m-m-m-m-m-m-m swans and humans

———

so cold so cold and hungry and cold
so cold so cold and hungry and cold

———

rosemeat and troutmash, blueberry ice cream with sheep sorrel
cabbage soufflé and worm pasta, cone mousse and berry jam
m-m-m-m-m-m-m swans and humans

———

so full and sated so full and happy
so full and sated and happy
m-m-m-m-m-m-m swans and humans

———

cold so cold so cold so cold so warm so cold so warm
full and hungry worm fingers and mudsicles
spring onion patties and salad
m-m-m-m-m-m-m swans and humans

Kornlilja brushed my hair and placed on my head a flower crown made of snowdrops, which were the first flowers to stick their noses out of the ground in the spring. María took my glasses and crushed them. The leader sat on the pink cushions and said: 'The distance no longer matters, Miss Elísabet Eva, daughter of Unnur and Rúnar.'

'Do not be afraid, Miss Elísabet Eva, for we know what we will do,' said Ástríður Petra. 'We are not going down without a fight and we are not indifferent to our fate.'

Blíng sang:

'Don't be afraid, I'm afraid on everyone's behalf, don't be afraid, I'm afraid on everyone's behalf, we are not going down without a fight and we are not indifferent to our fate like so many who don't give a shit shit shit shit shit shit,' she laughed, 'shit shit, we are just girls who only know how to make themselves feel good, just girls, girls who don't not give a shit, not give give give a shit no but thanks anyway.'

María cleared her throat and sang loudly like she was asking both the moon and the stars for an audience:

'The stars are not stars but shards of glass. The stars are not stars but shards of glass and the shards are stars.'

Blíng sang:

'Fear not, fair maiden, for I shall devour the fear like butter, not give a shit; we will look after you and fear on your behalf, do not be afraid afraid afraid afraid afraid do not give a shit afraid doesn't matter shit doesn't matter do not be petrified, you obsequious girl.'

'I am not petrified,' I mumbled.

'Of course she is petrified,' sang María.

'Of course you are petrified,' sang Blíng.

'The hatchling is born,' I said.

'Thank you for letting us know,' someone whispered in my ear, then someone else stamped better on my glasses. Captivated, I listened to the crunch of broken glass and fell asleep in Kornlilja's arms.

They sang:

the stars abandon their grief
the stars abandon their grief and step down to earth
and step down to earth in glass shoes with their glass knives
and glass eyes

Operation

The walking motion lulled me to sleep and woke me, lulled me, woke me, lulled. They bore me aloft, five or six or seven of them. The stars that shone in the sky morphed into flowers. From the ground sprouted flowers on stalks as tall as men and their coronas took on the appearance of stars. The swanfolk transported me aboard a boat. I listened to the sighing of oars while the stars in the sky sprinkled colours over the water. As the colours touched the surface, stars on tall stalks sprouted up out of the water and quivered in the gentle breeze. The bodies of the rowers were as slim as the stalks, and their arms resembled leaves, their heads calyxes, and their pistils joined in the singing of the swanfolk who sat around me in the boat as I lay:

row row rowww
the soil absorbs blood
row row rowww
the soil absorbs blood blood
row row rowww
the soil absorbs blood trail blood

row row rowww
the soil absorbs blood flood

Two swanladies or swanblokes – in this bird realm there was no such thing as ladies or blokes but still one marked the difference and still one didn't mark a difference and still one marked a difference – stroked my cheek, and nimble fingers braided my hair like no one had ever braided my hair, to the rhythm of the rowing and the song and the waves while we sailed over the water. The distance I sensed as being on a par with that of the world's longest lake.

While I slept I must have been carried ashore, because I woke surrounded by bushes and trees in the same night, which everywhere was decorated with dim blossoms and bright stars – in the sky, the earth, and the trees in equal measure. An operation was performed on me that I did not understand:

I lay fully clothed in the nest and sensed that the jumper and coat kept me warm and that my feet and arms were restrained in shackles. A cold bag was inserted into my womb through my vagina. If I tried to get up, a hand pushed me down and indecipherable words were whispered in my ears. Another hand cupped my forehead and stroked over and around my eyes.

'Calm yourself,' said a voice I didn't recognise, but instead I stiffened and screamed. A third or fourth or fifth palm smothered the scream. Despite the training I had received as a new recruit in carrying foreign objects inside my body, I wanted to cry. During those same years I received training in not crying: never in the company of enemies, never in the company of friends – for they could turn out to be enemies and enemies could turn out to be friends – and not in private. Of all my training, this proved the most beneficial to me, speaking as the person that I was in this moment but who disappeared in that place, if it could be called a place at all. María's breath brushed my ear, then she whispered:

'One day each and every one of us will be forced to sacrifice herself for love.'

Then her touch quickly turned to harm as she twisted my ear, then let go.

The sky offered me an ever more beautiful and colourful field of flowers whenever the hand covering my eyes lifted. Another hand squeezed my lips. Someone held my genitals and labia in order to fasten inside me a carton or box or bag, which the body began to warm on the inside. I struggled in the ropes until I lost consciousness and lay nowhere.

How do I draw a treasure map of this *nowhereland* one goes to and returns from with hands full of nothing and time at negative coordinates?

I probably didn't wake up right away.

I felt I slept an age in the clutches of intangible talons, then slumbered unconsciously, finally drifted in a haze. When I awoke I was lying on the green bench by the green lake and was shivering underneath a desertlike, blown-up and fragmented sky.

Goddess in a Red Leather Jacket

I slipped down the night and landed at the bottom of morning, trembling and shivering. I was cold. I was hungry. I couldn't move. I was too cold to sit still. Everything around me was out of focus. The birds slept. When I asked the sky and earth what I could do, the former answered:

'Nothing.'

'Nothing,' answered the earth after a moment's thought.

The water slept, and the bushes.

I clambered onto the road, stumbled along the hard shoulder. At lightning speed a red sports car approached and braked suddenly. The gust of air brushed my coat and my cheek. A person reached across the passenger seat and opened the door. On her head she wore a golden crown encrusted with glimmering red stones. Long brown fingers with golden nails grabbed the gearstick when I had sat down. We drove off. A goddess straight as an arrow sat behind the wheel wearing a red leather jacket over a grey, possibly polka-dot jumper.

'Where are you coming from?' said the goddess, reaching into the back seat and handing me a blanket, which I wrapped around me.

'Nowhere.'

'Shall we drive up to the rape crisis centre?' she said, and shot me a glance.

'No, I'm just happy to be myself again, though I didn't exactly miss myself while I dwelled offstage.'

'I don't understand what you're saying, but I don't need to understand everything,' she said, fixing her eyes on the road.

'Precisely,' I replied, and leaned back in the seat.

The car glided melodiously along the worm-soft road. The interior smelled of leather, smoked whisky, wild thyme – the aromas made my eyelids heavy. From a distance I heard the goddess ask a question, which I never answered. Then I half woke, pointed to a cluster of buildings, asked whether this was the industrial area by the harbour and would she stop here. The car bumped sweetly into the kerb. Could I get home without assistance? Oh yes, that I could. Rex sat waiting for me on the bench in the bus shelter, then disappeared out of sight.

Selma

She stood in my kitchen on the wine-red mat that I had bought as a shield from the cold floor, the circles under her eyes purple like the apron around her hips, holding my grandmother's yellow spatula in one hand. In a pan she fried eggs – sunny side up – wearing a blue mesh dress, barefooted in sandals that she must have brought from home (size 5.5, mine 8.5). We had bought ourselves sandals while attending a NATO conference on information technology in Athens a few years back. We performed a quick weapons check on each other. The formality took only a moment in the hands of professionals. Her hips had narrowed. Selma looked into my eyes as she felt my hips and the front of my waistband. I did not return the look, went and found my old glasses, took off my socks and put on my sandals (size 8.5). She asked why the electronic tag was missing from my ankle. I had no idea and showed her the imprint – there it was. Unprompted, she said that she had not made use of the grace period to think it over – what grace period? – Rósa and Venus were no more, she was no longer interested in being tied down – 'Being tied down?' – 'Yes, I want to be free like you,' she asserted and waved the yellow spatula, flung the eggs from the pan onto blue Russian dishes I had bought in Israel – she had bought the same dishes, in a wine-red colour if I recall. I loved the verb *to assert*. A person who had no need for the love of people loved words.

The coffeepot whistled – *whoo whoo whoo* – this is what you call perfect timing, all thanks to my boss's stellar command of time, and in this moment – *whoo whoo whoo* – in a yellow house on a brown hill above a blue cove, which cut into a beautiful blue bay beside a violet mountain, I felt a feeling that called forth in me simultaneously the sister words *anticipation* and *excitement*. How I looked forward to seeing Selma grow old and lose her command of time. She would be as winsome as an old funambulist who clambers up onto the back row of the circus, sits there like an acrophobic dove and watches the next show.

On the dining table my boss had spread a purple cloth and placed upon it a vase made of blue glass filled with snowdrops from the field nearby where Rex frolicked undisturbed. The blue Russian dishes from the ceramics store in Tel Aviv floated onto the table. Dim red coffee ran into the dim blue coffee cups, but I can't remember anymore where we bought those, on the occasion of which conference. Before catching a glimpse of her hips I closed my eyes.

'I love Sundays,' Selma declared. 'Won't you take off your coat?' she added, and suddenly I feared that were I to take the coat off I would blow up: I felt it was made of tinder.

Selma sat down, grabbed her yellow napkin, unfolded it, and laid it in her lap. She performed each action in the right sequence and never got confused about the order. One always came before two. Two always before three. She would never mix up the numbers. Unless she were to grow old. How I looked forward to that. I, on the other hand, forgot to unfold my napkin before I picked up the fork. And which was I meant to pick up first, the fork or the knife? It must be more peaceable to pick up the fork first. The alternative might be construed as a declaration of war. I had completely failed to learn table manners from Selma and had not paid proper attention to Grandma's lessons either despite my innate attention to detail, which subsequently received the best and most technical training an attention span could get in my country.

'Where have you been, my love?' she asked.

'Selma, we contribute directly to the injustice in the world,' I replied.

'That's true, Frankó,' said Selma.

Then we ate fried eggs with bread topped with soft French butter, which had been on sale last time I had gone out to the grocery store, but I just couldn't for the life of me remember when that shopping trip took place, I who had a memory of steel and was trained to utilise it strategically. But my memory still wasn't as good as Mum's. Hopefully Æsa had inherited it. The butter hadn't aged half a day. Selma said she was glad to get me back alive. I looked up under the chandelier to God Almighty's hiding place, then at the table: it would be nice if the food on the plates never finished and the moment didn't pass – and it appeared it wouldn't, something refused to give way.

'Do you feel very nauseated?' said Selma, scrutinising me like a spy.

'Yes,' I replied.

'I bought you a nightdress decorated with anchors, with a red bow on the collar. You are so fond of bows. Don't you like bows?'

'Yes,' I replied.

'Aren't you going to take off your coat, darling?'

'Not until the threat has passed.'

'What threat?'

POSTSCRIPT

BRUNCH
29 May

Hótel Absalón

On Sunday, 29 May, the Special Unit came together re-
newed and in good health for brunch at Hótel Absalón,
which served the best brunch buffet in town – the price included as much orange juice in sparkling wine – mimosas, they
were called – soft drinks, coffee and tea as you could drink.
We had all undergone our annual physical and the nation's top
psychiatrists had analysed workplace morale and measured our
individual mental aptitude. We were also celebrating the golden
plover's arrival to the East Fjords, late in the year though it was,
and the trees' new complement of spring-green leaves. At the
Norwegian Independence Day celebrations the results of the
apocalottery had been announced and my ticket had come up:
a three-person tent + a camping set for four.

Selma Mjöll, who sat at one end of the table, stood up, welcomed us, and announced that she would no longer be acting as
the motherly force in the unit's management, but would remain
in her post as a responsible autonomous individual. She gestured
toward Helgi Björn, who sat at the other end of the table, and
explained that he, too, would no longer take a fatherly role in

the office, that all the employees of the unit, including the superiors, were orphaned, metaphorically speaking, and would have
to take full and independent responsibility for themselves and
their actions. So dawned the new era of responsibility and trust,
fuelled by a radical revision of existing values and democratic
reform. She and Helgi Björn would continue to be superiors in
name but not in action. Everything was heading in a proper and
more prosperous direction. Helgi Björn nodded in agreement.
We clapped our hands, lifted our glasses, and said cheers. Selma
sat down and Nói Ingason rose to his feet, addressed the group,
was happy to see us all together and in one piece after a difficult
winter, lifted his glass and looked in my direction:

'Cheers to Elísabet Eva, welcome back to our wonderful
workplace.'

'Thank you,' I replied.

'May you recover from the trials and tribulations of the past
and do well in your new lot as an expectant mother. Cheers,
dear Elísabet.'

'Thank you,' replied Elísabet.

'Our relations at the Special Unit have always been amen-
able and, all things considered, perfectly good. Our experience
bears it out, and all the expert research demonstrates conclu-
sively that the Special Unit is an exceptionally good workplace,'
added Nói. 'Let us not allow that to change. Let that which is
good keep its course. Thank you, Helgi Björn and Selma Mjöll,
for having managed the Special Unit better than one could have
imagined it was possible to steer a workplace that handles such
dangerous and delicate matters.'

He lifted his glass, we all lifted our glasses, said cheers and sipped our mimosas. Nói cleared his throat and said:

'Dear bride-and-groom-to-be, Axel and Lóa, would you be so kind as to ask Elísabet Eva's forgiveness for having diligently executed the orders of your superiors on a rather beautiful sunny day in our city and taken Elísabet Eva out of commission by way of a dubious incursion into her body? And may I invite our superiors, Helgi Björn Björnsson and Selma Mjöll Ófeigsdóttir, to ask Elísabet Eva's forgiveness for not having trusted her better in the heat of the moment, at a turbulent juncture, even though according to our training we employees of the unit should, above other employees in the country, endure strain better than most. And last but not least, may I ask you, Elísabet Eva, kindly to forgive your colleagues and superiors their human fallibility?'

Axel and Lóa, Helgi Björn and Selma Mjöll, all formally asked for my forgiveness. Their requests did not hang long in the air. Words don't like to overstay their welcome. I bowed my head and said:

'You are all readily forgiven. Cheers.'

It would be an easy route from the table to the restroom. Around a corner and to the side behind a smaller hall there stood in a row four aubergine-coloured doors leading to equally many toilet bowls, the facilities exemplary, rolled-up white washcloths by marble hand basins with gold taps. Alongside us in the hall, large families were celebrating milestones. Dressed-up children ran between tables. Couples alternated carrying yellow and pink travel cots in and out of the room.

Watchful family elders sat at the heads of long rectangular tables, but our table was oval-shaped and thus smaller than the others in the hall. Nói asked us for a round of applause and then to please eat, better to be invited to herbs with love than to a fatted calf with hatred, he laughed and sat down. On my plate lay scrambled eggs.

'One of the atoms within us is God,' said Kristinn Logi, 'according to the latest research. That's why God is always so close, and why it is so difficult to rise up against him – it's like protesting oxygen or attacking oneself.'

He waved his knife before cutting a sausage in half.

'God is one's conscience,' Nói replied, waved his fork and stuck it into a mountain of pancakes smothered in syrup and cinnamon.

'But what about the goddesses, are they not atoms within us?' said Magnea.

'They never got that far,' replied Kristinn Logi.

'Before God abandoned the earth,' explained Nói, 'he left a part of himself behind as an atom, but humankind always pushed back against the goddesses and in response to this mistrust the goddesses began developing viruses. They're still at it.'

'For revenge?' asked Magnea.

'So they still live on Earth?' asked someone else.

'I don't understand this,' said Lóa and stuck her fork in her dimple, 'are the gods male and the goddesses female, no intersex or asexual gods?'

'See here, Lóa,' said Kristinn Logi, schoolmaster-like. 'Mankind named the gods and goddesses *gods* and *goddesses*. They themselves never revealed anything about their sex or gender and have never themselves told us their real names.'

Lóa asked her fiancé to taste a bacon-wrapped date. Axel accepted and offered Lóa a grape.

'The goddesses still live in a faraway realm, some leftover corner of the dimension that humans otherwise seized as their own, no one knows where,' explained Nói. 'I forgot to tell you the other day that the goddesses themselves had an internal dispute. The fertility goddesses did formidable work in the proliferation of humankind and had women who didn't want children murdered.'

Lóa was visibly startled. She belonged to a lobbying group that defended the rights of women who were unable, or chose not to have children.

'Yes,' replied Nói, holding a strawberry, 'the goddesses of pleasure and parties challenged the goddesses of celibacy to a duel on a large battlefield. Neither side won, but for a long time afterwards mankind didn't know how to have fun or be content with anything. The forest nymphs declared sex to be hazardous, that people ought to eat good food, take walks and go swimming, take in the aroma of plants and trees, listen to music in the winter in the embrace of dogs and calves. The goddesses of sex formed a coalition with the goddesses of wine, who later broke the treaty. The goddesses of love were held captive in a joint coup by the fertility goddesses and the goddesses of economy.'

Selma Mjöll never looked in Helgi Björn's direction. Helgi Björn never looked in Selma Mjöll's direction. Rósa and Venus had left them. Frankó would, if there was time, and in order to ensure the secret language didn't die out, write letters in the secret language on pink stationery in order to read them later on, privately, at night by the living room window.

'Do you all remember the lecture given by the psychiatrist who said that we couldn't embrace love until we loved equally the murderer and the casualty, the perpetrator and the victim, extinct species as well as humankind?' said Axel, who polished the syrup from his plate with a pancake.

'Ew, I would not like to reconcile with my murderer,' protested Lóa, who polished the syrup from her plate with a pancake.

'Me neither,' protested Kristinn Logi.

'Or a rapist,' protested Magnea, and ate an olive.

'I hate violence,' protested Nói, and dabbed his lips.

'I just remember the lecture on strategies for combatting depression, which included washing your face with cold water five times a day, sitting down in a peaceful spot once a day, closing your eyes and thinking about something sad for ten minutes, and walking by the ocean once a week and taking in its beauty,' Magnea said.

'This was the same lecture, Magnea,' Úrsúla pointed out, waving a fork.

'One person remembers one thing, the other something else,' said Lóa and wiped her fingers with her napkin.

Úrsúla: 'I tried for ten days to wash my face five times a day with cold water, think about something sad for ten minutes, but the feelings started to seem fake. I no longer believed my feelings, I milked myself for tears. I hate that.'

'I hate that too,' I agreed, but didn't know exactly what I hated. Fakery, violence, pretense, myself –

'I just remember a lecture where we were advised to act like an animal for half an hour a day, both in thought and action, and I took a bath and pretended to be a duck,' Lóa said.

'Is utopia already upon us?' said Nói and looked back and forth between Helgi Björn and Selma Mjöll, who grabbed her napkin.

'I'm telling you,' Magnea said and raised her index finger, 'it's easier to hate than to love, because in the hatred you never have to look yourself in the eye.'

'I find it easier to love than to hate,' said Lóa, and took her fiancé's hand.

'But it *is* harder,' insisted Magnea.

'Much harder,' Kristinn Logi agreed.

'I see no difference,' said Úrsúla.

'Then I ate so many prawn sandwiches every day that I had to go to a clinic.'

Said someone.

I placed my napkin on top of the scrambled eggs and walked out of the hall, opened a dark-purple door.

Dear time, I beg you

                    not

                         to watch over me

or cure me of shame.

penguin.co.uk/vintage